A Pure Clear Light

✳

Also by Madeleine St John

The Women in Black
The Essence of the Thing
A Stairway to Paradise

A Pure Clear Light

a novel

Madeleine St John

CARROLL & GRAF PUBLISHERS, INC.
NEW YORK

Copyright © 1996 by Madeleine St John

First Carroll & Graf edition 2000

Carroll & Graf Publishers, Inc.
19 West 21st Street
New York, NY 10010-6805

Library of Congress Cataloging-in-Publication Data is
available.
ISBN: 0-7867-0756-9

Manufactured in the United States of America

For my sister

I

'Simon, there's a woman over there who keeps looking at us.'

'Surely not.'

'There *is*. For God's sake; take a look yourself. It must be someone you know.'

'Hardly likely, darling. Just your imagination.'

'I haven't *got* any imagination, as you perfectly well know. Look, there she goes again. Hurried, furtive glances. Oh my God.'

Simon shrugged. 'It's probably Flora,' he said.

Gillian pulled her hand away from Simon's 'That was despicable,' she said.

And so it was: for Flora was Simon's deceived, betrayed wife, and Gillian was his mistress, and whether or not their liaison itself was in poor taste (as some might have averred) flippant or jesting remarks very surely were. Simon's expression was all contrition; shame filled his heart. 'Sorry, darling,' he said. 'Sorry, sorry, sorry.'

Gillian said nothing. It was Flora to whom the apologies were actually due: strange that it should be she who should apparently be more conscious of this. She picked up her glass and drank, glancing across the crowded brasserie as she did so. Simon saw her sudden startled glance. 'There she goes again,' she hissed. 'For heaven's sake, Simon, take a look yourself. Look in the mirror.'

Gillian was sitting with her back to the wall, which was

lined with mirror glass; Simon, opposite her, peered into its depths. 'Such a lot of people,' he said. 'Where is she sitting, exactly?'

'Over by the door. In a black hat. You should spot her easily.'

Simon looked again, and this time he saw the hat: he saw the hat, he saw – briefly, dreadfully, and just sufficiently – the face beneath it. 'Oh my God,' he said. And he seemed to shrink down in his chair, as if wishing to extinguish himself entirely.

'Who is it?'

'Of all the putrid, idiotic bad luck.'

'Who *is* it?'

'Don't look now,' Simon said, 'for God's sake, don't look now – in fact, don't look again, ever. She mustn't know we've seen her. There's just a chance that she won't be sure it's me. After all, she's only seen my back.'

'Unless she's seen your face in the mirror,' said Gillian. 'Who the hell is she, Simon?' Gillian was terrified that it might, indeed, be Flora, whom she had never seen, whom she hoped she might never, never see; she was appalled at the idea in any case of their having been seen, she and Simon together: that some innocent explanation might just conceivably be offered and accepted for their presence here, now, was almost beside the point. And what, so far, had the unknown woman seen – their clasped hands? the veil of intimacy which enclosed them here in this crowded place? Who, in any event, *was* she?

'Well, it isn't Flora,' said Simon.

'Thank God for that.'

'But it's almost as bad. Almost.'

'Which is?'

'It's Lydia. It's Lydia Faraday.'

'And who, *exactly*,' said Gillian, 'is Lydia Faraday?'

2

When Simon had first known Flora – a decade and a half ago: how time flew! – she had still been a professing Roman Catholic, but he had soon talked her out of it.

'I can't believe no one has told you all this before,' he said, having itemised the horrid ingredients in that scarlet brew – moral blackmail, misogyny, cannibalism and the rest. 'At Cambridge, or wherever.'

'Oh, but they have,' Flora assured him.

'But?'

'I didn't really care,' said Flora, 'what the others said.'

'Ah,' said Simon. He was home and dry. They got married, when the time eventually came, in an Anglican church, causing sorrow and consternation to Flora's parents, who knew in their bones that this was not a proper marriage ceremony, and joy and satisfaction to Simon's, whose bones told them that no other – truly – was; although of course by 'proper' they meant something rather different from what Flora's parents meant; but since the bride's mother is expected to cry, anyway, everyone looked as happy on the occasion as they ought.

When they had been married for several years, and Flora began to get a brooding look now and then, and to ask rhetorical questions about spiritual growth, Simon took a stern line. 'For heaven's sake,' he said.

'Exactly,' said Flora.

'Look,' said Simon, 'we're not going to have to go through this again, are we? It's hocus pocus. You agreed. And there are the kids to consider.' They had two girls and a boy.

'Yes,' said Flora. 'I'm considering them.'

'They can be Anglican if they like,' said Simon expansively. 'You too, for that matter. Further than that I'm not prepared to go. Honestly, Flora. I mean it, the Pope and Days of Obligation and plastic Virgin Marys with light bulbs inside them and all the rest of it – no way. Not in my house. *Please*. It's just too effing *naff*.'

Flora looked down at the floor to hide her smile, but despite herself, she began to laugh. Yes, Days of Obligation, the Pope – it was naff, alright. But then – what could you expect? Simon was laughing too, relieved and glad. But then Flora stopped laughing. 'That's not the whole story,' she said. 'After all.' Simon didn't want to go into the rest of the story, the part that wasn't naff, because that was something even worse.

'Be an Anglican,' he reiterated. It was the lesser of two evils. In fact it was hardly evil at all; it was probably completely harmless. 'No naffery there.'

'I wouldn't be too sure about *that*,' said Flora.

She let the whole thing ride for another year, but when the mood once more came upon her – or was it the Holy Ghost speaking to her? Probably – she looked again at the noticeboard in the porch of an Anglican church not too far from where they lived in Hammersmith, and judging it rightly to be High (another, nearer, was Low) she found herself noting the times of the masses. Hmmmm, she thought. She had no present intention of attending; she was just sussing it out. In any case, she was too busy to brood very often, because she had gone into business with a woman friend importing and selling third-world textiles; and the children continued to be highly labour-intensive: Janey was thirteen, Nell was nine, and little Thomas had just turned five.

3

Simon was not beset by brooding questions about spiritual growth – the Holy Ghost, it appears, was content to leave him to his own devices – but he had reached a point of vague disquiet with the givens, that was a fact. Simon had meant originally to become the Jean Renoir *de nos jours*, but actually he directed television plays and not especially meritorious ones at that. He was gritty and impatient and competent and personable and always had plenty of work; there was never time to sit down quietly and write the script of another *Grande Illusion*. He had a family to care for after all, Flora's income notwithstanding: and that was earmarked for the school fees, anyway. So Simon just got on with it – and it wasn't such a bad old life; there were lots worse. Flora was looking a bit seedy these days, but you had to expect that. The children were pretty, and clever: they argued a lot – you had to expect that, too – but he could tell from the manner of their arguing that they had sharp wits, so their futures in this jungle of a world seemed (as far as they could be) secure.

He nevertheless believed that one of these days, soon, he would find a window in the schedule, and would fly through it into a warm well-lighted place in which that script (a production certainty) could and would be written; or at any rate, started.

It was just six months or so after Flora had noted – and

then forgotten – the times of the Sunday and weekday masses that something resembling a window seemed to appear in the wall around Simon, in that he found he would not after all be able to accompany Flora and the offspring to the *gîte* in the Périgord which they had taken with some friends of theirs – the Hunters, and their two sons – during the summer holidays. It had been intended that he would join them for a fortnight of the scheduled month but this was now impossible: a job which ought to have been finished in time had had to be deferred, and Simon was therefore, as he explained to Flora, 'Fucked.'

'Oh dear,' said Flora, rather relieved at the thought of being away from him for a bit. 'Poor Simon.'

'Yeah,' said Simon. He was in fact thinking that, with no family around him to distract his attention and commandeer his time, he might be able, at last, to sit down and get to work on that script. The longer one left these things the better they potentially became, but it really was time to get cracking, because *he wasn't getting any younger.*

4

Hail Mary, full of grace, the Lord is with thee, said Flora under her breath, and the Virgin Mary (all lit up from inside, as if by an electric light bulb) inclined her head ever so slightly. She was ready to receive whatever further confidences Flora might have. *What did you wish to say to me, my child?* Blessed art thou among women, and blessed is the fruit of thy womb, Jesus. *Yes, yes. And?* Holy Mary, Mother of God, pray for us sinners now and at the hour of our death. *Very good, Flora: I will pray for you.* Ever-ready, ever-virgin mother of God – pray for my children! *Certainly.* And Simon, my husband. *It shall be done.*

Flora picked up the paring knife and went on with the dinner preparations. She didn't sufficiently believe in God – believe? in God? what could this possibly, now, mean? – to pray to him, or Him, or, just conceivably, Her – but the Virgin was a tolerant sort of creature: nothing if not tolerant: look what she'd put up with already! so there was no difficulty about asking her to do the praying for one. That was what mothers were for. Hail Mary, full of grace, she began again; and the front door slammed shut and Simon came in. The light went out inside the Virgin Mary and she faded from view. 'Oh, hello darling,' said Flora; 'how was your day?'

'Pretty vile. What about you?'

'Oh, fine, fine. My day was *fine*.'

'Oh well. Have we got any gin?'

'Could you just go and sort out the kids first – there's an arbitration matter. I left it for you.'

'Those bloody kids. Where are they?'

'Upstairs. No, Janey's in the sitting room. You'll find them soon enough if you look. Go on.'

He went away, muttering, but came back looking pleased with himself. 'I've sorted it,' he said.

'Good.'

'I had to bribe them.'

'Did it cost much?'

'A fiver.'

'No one could say we haven't taught them the value of money.'

'No, they could not. Where's that gin?'

Holy Mary, Mother of God.

'I was thinking, so long as you can't come to France – is that really off, Simon? Definitely? – I was thinking, I might ask Lydia if she'd like to come with us.'

'What?'

'Lydia. You know, Faraday. Lydia Faraday.'

'Yes, I know who you mean. Lydia Faraday. What on earth do you want to ask Lydia Faraday for?'

'Well, why ever not? Poor Lydia.'

'Poor *hell*.'

'Simon!'

'Well, for God's sake.'

'Anyway, what's it to do with you? You won't be there.'

'Oh, *Flora*.' Simon sprawled back in his armchair and clutched his head. 'Honestly,' he said. '*Lydia*.'

Flora, watching this performance, began to laugh.

'What have you got against poor Lydia?' she said. Simon let go of his head and sat up. He reached for the gin bottle and topped up his drink — Flora always made them too weak — and took a swallow.

'In the first place,' he said, 'she isn't *poor*. She's probably got more than the rest of us put together. Jack was saying —'

'Then he shouldn't have been,' said Flora severely. Jack Hunter, a solicitor, had done some work for Lydia a year or two back, when she had got into a tax muddle.

'Don't be priggish,' said Simon. 'The point is, Lydia likes to put it about that she's on her uppers, but —'

'That's not true either,' said Flora. 'I never heard her putting it about that she was short of money.'

'No, she doesn't say so in so many words,' said Simon. 'She's not that obtuse. She just suggests it in a thousand tiny ways. I could practically throttle her sometimes. Who's she trying to impress?'

'Simon, what are you talking about?' cried Flora, amidst her laughter. 'Name me even one of those thousand tiny ways.'

'Well, look at the way she dresses.'' said Simon, 'for a start.'

'Dresses?'

'Yes, *dresses.*'

'Fancy your noticing the way she dresses!' Flora had stopped laughing, or even smiling. What could this mean?

Simon scented the danger and rushed to avert it. 'I wouldn't *notice,*' he said, 'if she didn't simply demand one's attention every time you see her. Oh God. Those bits and pieces.'

'I always think Lydia looks very nice,' said Flora, whose own taste ran to French jeans and plain white T-shirts, and things from the Harvey Nick's sales for more formal occasions; 'for a woman of her age.'

'Miaow!' cried Simon, and they both laughed. One thing

which cemented their relationship was that gin always put them in a good humour; so generally they drank some every evening.

'And that's another thing,' said Simon.

'What is?' said Flora.

'Well, her age. I mean, Lydia: it was one thing when one first knew her; fair enough; loose cogs – you expect them when they're in their twenties, early thirties. Missed the first bus, but there'll still be a few more; but now, ten years or so later – well: precious few buses. Probably none. Probably missed the last one. And there she still is loose-cogging around the scene, just getting in the way – it's embarrassing.'

Flora was appalled. 'Well, really!' she exclaimed. 'How – '

'And then she has to make a meal of it,' said Simon, 'with all those jumble-sale outfits. And that itty-bitty flat of hers. And she always wants a lift. She's just so *pointless.*'

'Mother of God,' said Flora.

'You what?'

'Mother,' said Flora. 'Of God.'

'What are you talking about?'

'Honestly, Simon. If you could hear yourself. The cruelty. That poor woman. What has she ever done to you?'

Simon had been recalled, unexpectedly, to sobriety. He considered the question. 'I dunno,' he said. 'She just depresses me.'

'Ah,' said Flora. 'Yes. I see. Yes. Make me another drink will you? There's just time for another before we eat.' She watched while Simon made the drink. Lydia *was* sometimes a bit of a downer, that was a fact; but she couldn't quite tell why. Oh, Mother of God: pray for us sinners.

5

When Flora had got herself married, and then Claire, and then Louisa – well, it rather left Lydia out in the cold, one could say: not that she seemed to care. Well, to be sure, it was – then – early days yet: it was a bit early for *caring*. But still: they (and Alison Brooke, who had vanished to New York, and who therefore did not in the same way thereafter count) had all been friends together, and it was a bit tricky, insofar as they still were, to keep Lydia in the frame when she had no husband or other partner. It was not such a fag while she was still youngish, and attractive – ish! said Simon – but it got trickier by the year. And now she was forty-ish, and it required a certain breadth of vision even to pose the question of whether or not she was, still, attractive. Ish!

'Attractive? Lydia? You must be joking!' said Simon.

'Oh, I don't know,' said Robert, husband to Louisa. 'She's not bad, is she?'

'If you go for that style of thing,' amended Alex, husband to Claire.

'Lydia is beautiful,' said little Thomas. 'I love Lydia.'

'Lydia has lovely clothes,' said Nell. 'She gets them from jumble sales. Can we go to a jumble sale, Mum?'

'Lydia is pathetic,' said Janey. 'Please don't ask her to come with us to France, Mum. She'll ruin everything.'

'How unkind you are,' said Flora. 'How do you mean, pathetic?'

'I don't know,' said Janey. 'She just is. She tries too hard.' People often did, with Janey, for she had a critical mien, but it was not a bit of use; it was indeed the worst thing one could possibly do. Janey was one very tough young woman.

Five years ago, when Thomas was a tiny baby, just home from the hospital, and Simon had had to go away on location for six weeks, Lydia had come to stay, because with Nell having been but four years old – although Janey was eight and reasonably self-sufficient – it was all a bit much for the rather flighty au pair: and Lydia had been – providentially, for the Beaufort household – between (as she so often, after all, was) jobs.

'But she's been absolutely wonderful,' cried Flora. 'I don't know what I would have done without her.'

Simon was always in an illish temper when he got back from one of these away-assignments, little new baby or no little new baby – 'See how much fatter he is since Daddy went away! Who's my fat little boy? Who's my little fatty? Who's Mummy's little darling! Who's this? This is your Daddy – yes, *Daddy* – smile for Daddy!'

Simon took the child and cuddled him, awkwardly at first and then with more aplomb, and said, over the baby's downy head, 'But really, Flora, she doesn't need to stay here any longer, does she, now that I'm back? I'd have thought she'd have been off out of the place by the time I fetched up – not installed in that kitchen with the girls making meringues as if she bloody lived here. When does she mean to go?'

The baby was becoming restless and Flora took him back. 'I don't know,' she said. 'She'll go soon, I expect. As soon as she gets the vibe you're giving out. Just carry on, Simon. Make her feel unwanted. I'll lay odds we'll see her calling for a taxi by suppertime.'

Simon ignored the irony in these remarks and simply asserted that he would be more than happy to take Lydia home himself. 'Where's she actually living these days?' he said.

'Oh, Maida Vale-ish,' said Flora vaguely. 'You know.' She had never actually been there.

'I don't,' said Simon, 'but I mean to find out.' He turned to leave the room.

'If you say even one word,' said Flora, 'to make her feel *de trop* I shall never have anything more to do with you.'

He was half out of the door but he turned back to face her. 'Now, would I do that?' he said.

He went down to the kitchen where Lydia and the eight-year-old Janey (looking fairly tough already) and the four-year-old Nell, all dressed in striped aprons, were sitting contemplating the meringues, all set out on a wire rack.

'We're waiting for them to get cold,' squeaked Nell. 'Then we're going to put whipped cream inside them, and then we're going to eat them!'

'I say,' said Simon. 'It's an orgy.'

'What's an orgy?'

He caught Lydia's dark brown (almost black) eye. 'It's a feast of pleasure,' he said drily.

'We're not going to eat them all,' said Janey very seriously. 'We're going to have one each. The rest are for pudding tonight.'

'Ah,' said Simon. Lydia stood up.

'Gabriella should be back any minute now,' she told him. 'There's a casserole in the oven for supper – she'll do the rest. So when we've finished this meringue business I'll begin making my way – as long as you don't need me for anything more here. I was actually just about to go up and sort this out with Flora when you came in. I'll go and do that now. See you in a minute, girls!' She left the room.

Oh God, thought Simon, she couldn't have overheard anything, could she? Surely not – they'd been two floors away. 'She's in the nursery!' he called out to her, as Lydia went up the stairs.

She returned ten minutes later. She looked perfectly happy. No, she couldn't possibly have overheard us, Simon assured himself. 'Right,' she said, 'that's all fixed. Simon, Flora told me that I must ask you if you'd mind taking me home – but for my part I must say that I wouldn't dream of troubling you; I can get a taxi easily.'

'We won't hear of it,' said Simon. 'My pleasure. When did you want to leave?'

'Well, Flora insisted on my staying for supper,' said Lydia. 'So after that, whenever you like. I'll just go and pack up, anyway – we'll do the meringues after that, girlies, okay? See you in a bit.' And she went off again. And then Gabriella turned up, and the evening programme proceeded on its way, until, finally, the moment arrived for Simon to take Lydia home to Maida Vale.

6

It wasn't what Simon would have called Maida Vale, but what the hell, here in any event they were, in a battered little street near the canal. 'Hmmm,' said Simon, looking up at the peeling façades of a terrace of ungentrified stucco-fronted houses; 'interesting neighbourhood. I don't believe I've ever been in this part of the world before.'

And if I have anything to do with it, Lydia's glance seemed to say, you won't again. 'Oh, really?' she said, in the surprised tone of one to whom the remark might have been uttered in, say, Gloucester Road. 'Well, never mind. You're here now. Thank you so much for the lift. I do hope you'll be able to find your way out again without too much trouble.' She'd had to give him directions towards the end.

'Oh, no problem, no problem,' said Simon. 'But look, you must let me give you a hand with that suitcase. Didn't you say you lived on the top floor?' The offer was purely a formality; the idea of entering the house was entirely unsympathetic: even fearsome. That peeling paint; God knew what rot might be found within.

'Oh, thank you,' said Lydia. 'How very kind.' Simon, flabbergasted, picked up the suitcase and followed Lydia – who was carrying two bulging plastic bags – through the front door and up the uncarpeted stairs.

It seemed clean enough, even sound enough; the landings

16

were free of refuse, needles, rats, and worse; there were no disgusting esoteric odours. It was a case of arrested decline rather than outright decay. They reached the top floor, and Lydia did the business with the mortice lock and at last opened her front door. 'Here we are,' she said. 'Do come in.' He could hardly refuse; filled with a new dread, he entered Lydia's flat.

Lydia had darted across the room on to which the front door immediately opened and turned on a desk lamp, and Simon, still carrying the suitcase, beheld a sitting room with three arched windows which overlooked the street. He put the suitcase down and glanced around at the shabby furniture, the haphazard décor. 'So this is where you live,' he said pointlessly.

'Yes,' Lydia agreed. She folded her arms and looked at him; she seemed to be smiling, half at him (at him, not with him) and half to herself: a smile which seemed challenging, ironical, mysterious, and almost – had it not suddenly vanished – infuriating. Who the hell are you, he might almost have said, to smile at me like that?

'Let me offer you a drink before you go,' she said, and she turned before he could refuse and looked inside a Victorian sideboard affair. 'I'm sure I've got something here, some-where.' He stood there, helpless, while she rattled bottles, and then she stood up, holding one aloft. 'How about this?' she said.

It was a bottle of green Chartreuse. Well, what else should it have been? 'Just a very small one,' he said.

'Of course.' She poured out two liqueur glasses full and handed him one. 'Do sit down,' she said, nodding towards the sofa. It was very faded and threadbare, and was draped with a large silk-fringed shawl. Simon sat down at one end, but Lydia remained standing by the sideboard. It was hard to tell in this half-light, but she seemed to be staring at him — not rudely, but certainly, frankly, staring.

'Won't you join me?' he said, inclining his head towards the other end of the sofa. She said nothing but crossed the room and sat down.

He hadn't quite noticed before how well she moved: she had a firm, rhythmical tread, and when she sat, her frame folded, just so, her back very straight. Where could she have learned to do all that? She moved — now he came to think of it — now that he'd actually watched her, properly, for the first time in all these years of intermittent brief meetings — like one of those old-time actresses. Deportment. A nice old-fashioned word for a nice old-fashioned thing. She sipped at the drink. There was something just right about the way she did that, too. Who, now he came to think of it (he must once have been told, but he hadn't actually been listening), *was* she? *Who are you, Lydia?*

'Have you lived here long?' he said, looking around the room again. Shabby didn't begin to say it: the curtains, for instance, were half in tatters, and the large Aubusson-style carpet on the floor was virtually threadbare — here and there you could just discern a rose-petal or two, the end of a blue riband, half a spray of foliage.

Lydia considered. 'I bought it three and a half years ago,' she said.

'Oh, you own it then.'

'Yes. My mother had one of her fits of conscience, and gave me the money.'

'Ah.'

'One of these days she may have another such fit, and I'll be able to do it up properly.'

'What about your father?'

'He has no conscience.'

'Your mother – '

'Lives in Australia. She ran off with an abstract expressionist when I was fourteen years old.'

Simon began to laugh, and then stopped. 'I am sorry,' he said. She shrugged. 'It doesn't matter,' she said.

'Your father, then – '

'My father's remarried and has another family; they all live in Bucks. I was my parents' only child. Now you know everything there is to know about me: I need only add that art is long and life is short – as I dare say you have already realised.' Her glance fell on him briefly, teasingly, dismissively. Now you can go, she might have said: and he was for the moment paralysed; he did not know how, politely, gracefully, to make a move. It was as if she had heard his unspoken question and had teasingly, then dismissively, answered it – but only to leave him wondering still further. *Yes, but who are you?*

He looked into his glass and then drained it and put it down on the low table in front of the sofa. 'I really must be going,' he said. 'Thanks for the Chartreuse.'

'That's alright,' she said. 'Thanks for the lift, and everything.'

He was standing up. It had all taken an almost superhuman effort; she rose in one swift, easy movement, like a bird taking flight, and walked over to the door and opened it. She stood, waiting for him to follow her and depart, her head slightly tilted. That smile again. He stood in the doorway, not twelve inches from her. She was almost as tall as he – much taller than Flora: her eyes almost directly met his. 'Well, good-bye,' he said. And, oh God, for one terrible instant he was seized by the impulse to lean forward and kiss her on the mouth; to extinguish that smile, subdue that teasing, alien glance. How could this be? He stopped himself just in time, of course.

But there was worse. For as he turned to go, finally, truly to depart, he saw that she had seen this impulse come and go, and thought as little of him for having resisted it as she would have thought of him for succumbing to it. He hastened down the stairs almost at a run, and escaped the terrible house. He did not see her again for another six months or so, and when he did, had all but forgotten that dreadful moment in the doorway: but looking at her at the other end of a dinner table – at the Carringtons, was it? – he thought, she's not my type at all, not remotely. Could she be anyone's?

7

Apparently not. Apparently no one wanted to hook up with Lydia. 'But how old exactly is she now? Thirty-five-ish?' Simon asked Flora, on the way home from that particular dinner party.

Flora was driving; Simon had been knocking back the Pinot Noir like no one's business. 'She's, well, a bit older than I am,' said Flora. 'She came up late to Cambridge: she went out to Australia for a few years after she left school.'

'Oh,' said Simon. He made no mention of his having heard the tale of Lydia's errant mother. You'd have thought his interest in the subject was nil. Well, and so it was.

'Her mother lives out there,' Flora went on. 'She has a gallery. In Sydney.'

'No kidding,' said Simon. Flora glanced at him. Well! It was, after all, he who had raised the topic of Lydia. 'Isn't it time old Lydia found herself a bloke?' he'd said, as they were driving along the embankment. 'She isn't *old*,' Flora had replied.

Simon thought, for one last moment, of Lydia: there was only one way to find out who she was, and he wasn't going to do so. He didn't even want to. Would anyone?

8

'All the same,' said Flora, 'I think I should ask her to come to France with us.'

'Please, Mum, *don't,*' said Janey. '*Please.*'

'She can sleep in my room,' said Nell. 'She can come with me.'

'Can Fergus come too?' asked Thomas. 'Can we ask Fergus to come to France with us? Fergus can sleep with me.'

'You won't even have room for her,' said Simon. A futile discussion ensued about the number and disposition of the beds and bedrooms at the *gîte*; 'I mean in the car, anyway. It'll be a squash as it is.'

'It would have been even squashier if you'd been coming,' said Flora.

'The whole advantage of my not coming,' said Simon, 'is that you won't be squashed in the car. Just think about it.'

'Can Fergus come?' Thomas asked again. 'Fergus won't squash.'

'She probably can't come anyway,' said Flora. 'She probably has too much to do here, at this time of the year.'

'Sure to,' said Simon. 'Leave her to get on with it.'

Lydia with advancing years and a receding economy had become unemployable, so had had perforce to employ herself: she was now the sole proprietor – and, indeed, employee – of Floating World Postcards Ltd, and had been trading, latterly at a small profit, for almost three years. The postcards depicted London in its more *insolite* aspects (she resorted to a small stable of freelance photographers, followers of E. Atget and A. Monnier and that ilk) and were gradually finding their way into the collections of the better class of tourist. 'I'll give her a ring, anyway,' said Flora weakly.

'*Please* don't ask her to come to France, Mum, said Janey. 'I do *implore* you.'

'Can Fergus come?' said Thomas again. 'Please, Mum, I do *implore* you.'

Flora, who was sitting to one side of him, and Nell, on the other, began to tickle him. 'No, you silly sausage,' Flora said. 'He can't. Fergus is going to Italy, so there!' Fergus Carrington! That was all they needed.

'Can we go to Italy?' asked Thomas.

This time everyone spoke with one voice. 'No,' they cried. '*We're* going to *France!*'

9

'If she'd got herself a bloke,' said Simon, 'the problem wouldn't arise.'

'Oh, Mother of God,' said Flora, taking off her make-up. '*If*.'

'What's all this Mother of God racket we've been hearing lately?' said Simon. He was lying in bed looking at a script.

'Oh, it's nothing,' said Flora.

'Then I wish you'd knock it off,' said Simon. 'It's making me nervous.'

'Why should it do that?'

'Well, since there's no such being as God, it's a bit too spooky by half to be hearing about the Mother of. Be reasonable.'

'Ah,' said Flora. 'Reasonable. *Raisonnable*. Well, who are we to know what's reasonable. Let alone *raisonnable*.'

'The very people,' said Simon. 'That's who.'

'Us sinners,' said Flora. '*We* sinners.'

'Yes, that's one of many possible appellations.'

'It's the most *raisonnable*.'

'Listen, Flora,' said Simon. 'I married you for your looks, not your brains.'

'I'm one seamless whole,' said Flora. 'Take it or leave it.' She got into bed.

'It's too late even to talk about leaving it,' said Simon. He

24

turned off the lamp and held her in his arms, still lying on his back, and kissed the top of her head. 'I'm stuck with it,' he said.

'Brains and all.'

'Yes,' he said. 'I'm doomed.' Flora said a few Hail Marys to herself, and fell asleep. Simon disengaged his arms, and turned over, and, after a while, fell asleep too.

10

Flora was thinking about the vast existential difference – it was, wasn't it? – between being right, and having, as the French say, right, or right-ness: *raison*: reason. There, rightness, or even righteousness, was reasonableness; and wrongness was therefore the consequence – or was it the condition? – of a logical error, a mistake. In French, to be right, *d'avoir raison*, was to have worked out a sum correctly, whereas in English there was no necessary suggestion of the reasonable: to be right in English was more like a piece of luck. Or a gift of God. Or a doom.

Flora was thinking about all this because she wanted to be right; the desire had arisen and was growing in her, she knew not why. The necessity was becoming almost urgent, whether to be right, or *d'avoir raison*, whichever it might more accurately be; and if it were a question after all of working out a sum correctly, then that would be existentially a rather different or even an entirely different affair from succumbing to a doom.

In any event, insofar as she could do the sum at all, or insofar as she could embrace her doom, Flora concluded that it would only be right to ask Lydia to come to France with them.

'Floating World, hello.'

'Oh Lydia is that you? Flora here.'

'Oh Flora, hello, how nice.'

'I know I mustn't keep you during working hours, you must be so busy – '

'So must you – '

'Yes, thank God, I suppose, it's just, I was wondering, are you going away this summer, have you anything planned?'

'Yes, I'm going down to Italy for ten days; I'm sharing that villa in Sardinia for a bit that the Carringtons have taken with Robert's sister, but she can't go down until after – anyway – so that's what I'm doing.'

'Ah. Yes, well – I'd been wondering whether you might like to come to France with us – Simon can't get away after all, you see, so we've some space – '

'Oh, so sorry, I would've loved to, but it's all settled now. You *were* sweet to think of me.'

'Couldn't you come on?'

'Now that would be flashy; how I wish; but I can't really leave the Floating World for that long, you see – not at this time of the year. It's really my busiest; it's like Christmas for Hamleys – '

'Oh, yes, of course, yes, obviously. Well – '

'Thank you anyway. It would have been lovely.'

'Oh, it's nothing. Sardinia will be lovely too.'

'I hope so. I've just been and bought a new cozzie.'

'You *are* brave!'

'Yes. I had a brandy first.'

'Did you really?'

'Yes, truly. And then I just marched into Horrids and got it.'

'Horrids, gosh.'

'They have such a huge selection.'

'That's a point.'

'And I couldn't face going from shop to shop to shop.'

'You are clever.'

'I could do with being thinner.'

'The swimming will see to that.'

'So I do hope. Darling I must go now, I have to telephone the printer.'

'Yes, right, I should be getting on with it myself, I'm doing the VAT returns. Have a lovely time in Sardinia if we don't speak again beforehand – '

'And you in – where, exactly?'

'The Périgord.'

'Oh how lovely.'

'We'll be in touch afterwards anyway, won't we?'

'Yes of course.'

They said their good-byes and Flora hung up. Well, so – she felt an odd sense of anti-climax. Honour on the one hand and selfish inclination on the other had both been satisfied: as so rarely can they be. Why then this odd sense of dissatisfaction?

She shrugged it off and went on with the VAT returns, but she could not quite divest herself of the feeling that God had been watching the whole affair from its inception, and was now laughing quietly to Himself: which, if there were no such person, was ridiculous, and, if there were such a person, was – what, exactly? She put down her pen and sat, speculating, for a moment. What, exactly, might one fairly expect the consequences of the Virgin's mediations to be – supposing, that is, that God existed? Had she been given a sign? She saw that this would not do: any further down that road, she thought, and I'll be back in the Middle Ages before I know it.

But then, she had in fairness to ask, is that, considering where we all now are, such a very dreadful destination? Flora felt suddenly a sense of the unmitigated grossness of the superstitions of the modern age. You could be crushed to death, if you weren't lucky. If you got the sum wrong. Hail Mary, she said, full of grace; *etcetera*. You could just conceivably get to a point, she thought, where it didn't matter whether or not God existed: where the possibility that He did, and might even listen to you, was absolutely all there was between you and hell. Because we do now know, at any rate, that hell exists.

I I

It was the night before Flora and the children were to leave for France.

'Will you be alright?'

'Of course I will.'

'You will eat properly won't you, I mean proper food, not canteen rubbish – '

'It isn't rubbish at all, it's jolly good nosh.'

'It isn't fresh. There's nothing raw.'

'There's salads.'

'Well, do make sure you eat them then, not just that overcooked junk.'

'It's good, that canteen stuff.'

'Sure, sure. And please don't forget Mrs Brick's wages, will you – I've left you a reminder on the bathroom mirror.'

'Right, right.'

'I think that's all.'

'Will *you* be alright?'

'Yes, of course.'

'Telephone me as soon as you get to Tours.'

'Will do.'

'And then when you get to the *gîte*.'

'Obviously.'

'You're taking all this far too calmly for my liking. After all, we've never done this before, you going off alone with the car and the kids.'

'Claire does it every year.'

'That's different.'

'Why?'

'Well, she and Alex don't – you know – '

'Whereas we do?'

'Don't we?'

'Of course. Of *course.*'

'Come here.'

Simon took Flora in his arms, sitting on the sofa, the television set still on but with the sound turned off. Flora leaned against him, her head on his shoulder, one arm loosely around his neck. After a while, 'Isn't life – but I can't find the word,' she said.

'I think I know what you mean.'

Flora tilted her head and looked up at him. '*What* do I mean?' she asked.

Simon pondered for a moment. 'Transitory,' he said. 'You mean *transitory.*'

'Oh.'

'Don't you?'

Flora considered the question. 'Ye-e-es,' she said. 'I *suppose* that's what I mean.' But there was something other, something more, or something, even, less, that she meant – in that strange and tiny space in the mind where it is just possible to mean without having the word which conveys that meaning. And one could not have said whether it were fatigue or fear which prevented her from searching for, and finding, the right word. The reasonable word. The *mot juste,* as English-speakers say.

12

Simon might not believe in the existence of God – indeed, he categorically did not – but he knew he was on the way to the great cutting-room in the sky nevertheless. He might not believe that a person called God was going to put him through the viewing machine and decide whether or not to save him or let him fall to the floor, but he had some sense nevertheless of there being some ineradicable rule by which this decision might – however purely theoretically – be made. He was on his way to a time, a place, where – when – this awful accounting would have occurred if there had been a person called God; that there was no such person did not alter the inexorability of the journey or of its theoretical destination. Simon had not idly given Flora the word she apparently sought: life was above all else transitory – oh, how tragically, yet fortunately, transitory! As the Wanderer (or was it the Seafarer? who could remember which was which!) had insisted: Just as that sorrow passed, so shall this.

In any event, you could hardly live in Hammersmith without being all but overwhelmed with the realisation of life's essential transience; the place was a monument to transience; and if that was a paradox, so much the better. Simon, in the family's absence, had taken to walking in the long summer evenings: one walked for a few miles, and then one came to a pub; one had a few pints and walked home again, and went to bed. One walked down impossible blighted streets, past lovely, blighted houses, the motorway roaring overhead, the river coming into view, every transient item supporting a stream of transient life: their only absolute reality was their passing.

Simon was looking out, tentatively, for locations for his script: he meant – tentatively – to tell the story which would reveal this tragic yet fortunate transience. It was the only story there now was; it was the only story that remained. He began to believe that he would stumble across the detail of the story as long as he just kept on walking. There would be – say – a house, in a row of others like it, in which the door would open: a woman would come out, and stand there for a moment at the top of the steps, uncertain –

directed by
SIMON BEAUFORT

and he might have found the house, the row of houses, seen the door open and the woman who came out and stood at the top of the steps – stunned by the sudden magnitude of the motorway traffic's roar – for a moment, uncertain, so soon as the end, say, of the first week of his solitude; might have begun to see the details of that story coming, slowly, then faster, into focus, might even have sat down and begun actually to write something (it was a long time since he'd actually written something: he could remember, just, what it felt like *to write*). He might have done all this were it not that, tragically, or perhaps fortunately – he couldn't, one couldn't, say which – the dinner invitations started to come in.

'Oh Simon you poor old thing. A whole month! Come round for a meal one night – let's see, what about Thursday?'

'Oh Simon I hear you're a grass widower – poor Simon!

Why don't you pop round here for a square meal one night – are you doing anything on Tuesday?'

For as everyone knows, men can, but don't, look after themselves when their wives are away, and it is one's duty – and, it must be admitted, one's pleasure – to give them a dinner or two. Poor Simon! He even found himself sharing the honours one evening with poor Alex – poor Alex Maclise, Claire being away – at the compassionate dinner table of the Ainsworths. 'I thought I might as well kill two birds,' said Lizzie to Alf. 'Poor old things.'

And it was at one such dinner table – this one, as it happened, in Camden Town – that Simon met a woman called Gillian Selkirk. The name alone ought to have been enough to warn him off: as Louisa Carrington was, much later, to observe to Robert of that ilk, 'It *writhes*. And so I dare say *does she*.'

13

Flora opened the shutters and looked down beyond the terrace, where Thomas was playing with some Lego, to the pool. Nell was sitting on the edge, dangling her feet in the water; Janey in a bikini was lying in the sun on a chaise longue. I should shout down and warn her not to stay in the sun too long, thought Flora.

She wondered vaguely where the Hunters could be, and then remembered that they had all – William and Denzil having found at the last minute urgent reasons of their own for doing so – gone into the village.

Flora had already had words with Janey on the subject of William Hunter, who was a year older than Janey and ought therefore to have been treated with the respect due to equals; but Janey would have none of it. 'He's a dork,' she told Flora, when upbraided for acting too much the little madam.

'He's nothing of the kind!' exclaimed Flora. 'He's a very nice, and I may say very intelligent young man. And if his manners weren't so good he wouldn't put up with your airs for five seconds flat.'

'There you are, then,' said Janey. 'He's a dork. I'm not saying he can *help* it. All the boys at that school are.'

'What could you possibly know about *all the boys* at that school,' said Flora. 'You, at your age.'

'*Everyone* knows about that school,' said Janey. 'It's absolutely famous for dorks; it always has been.'

'That school, miss,' said Flora, 'is one of the very best and most ancient not only in this country but in the world.'

'There you are then,' said Janey. 'Dork City.'

'If none of them will ever want to have anything at all to do with you, ever, said Flora, 'it will serve you right.'

'Suits me,' said Janey.

'I'll remember you said that,' said Flora. 'Now go away, and be nice to William. Just to prove how superior you truly are. We all know now how superior you can make yourself look; the point has been made more than adequately. Let's see how genuinely superior you are.' Her request was granted, but she came soon enough to wish that it had not been; that she had never made it; that Janey might not be so truly, one way or another, superior.

'Of course,' Janey said, accommodatingly, to her mother, 'they're probably all utterly dorky at that age. From what I've seen so far.'

'Possibly,' said Flora. 'If you insist on seeing them in that light. To me they just seem nice, if slightly awkward, well-meaning young men.'

Janey shrieked. 'Men!' she cried. 'I wouldn't call them *men!*'

Flora had to laugh. 'Well, whatever,' she said. 'I mean, you can't call them boys, it's too infantile.'

'No, they're not boys, and they're not men, they're *dorks*,' said Janey.

Flora was just about to shout out and warn Janey out of the sun when she saw two people whom Janey would unhesitatingly have termed dorks bicycling up the road. Dorks as they might be, they were now turning in at the driveway, and cycling towards the house. Flora stood watching, fascinated. Dorks they might in Janey's estimation be, dorks they might truly be: but brave new world, that had such dorks in't!

36

They were, as far as she could see from here, identical twins, and they were surpassingly beautiful: tall – albeit still evidently adolescent – slender, fair-haired and graceful. Having arrived at the *piscine* and sighted Janey on her chaise longue, they stopped cycling and stood lankily astride their machines. They looked at each other and shrugged interrogatively and one of them then spoke. 'Mademoiselle, s'il vous plait!'

Janey, aware for the first time of the intrusion, opened her eyes and sat up, staring, in a passable representation of the startled faun. 'Qu'est-ce que vous voulez?' she said.

'Ah!' exclaimed her interlocutor; 'you're *English!*' His companion smiled pleasantly. 'Do forgive us,' said he, 'for disturbing you, but we're looking for one William Hunter, whom we believe to be staying somewhere hereabouts. We thought this might be the house, but it seems we're mistaken. We'll leave you in peace. So sorry for the intrusion. As you were.'

They were on the point of pedalling away again when the astonished Janey found her voice. 'No, wait,' she said. 'This *is* the right house. William's just gone to the village. He'll probably be back soon. You could wait, if you like.'

14

Flora continued to stand just inside the window, where she could not easily be seen from below, and went on watching, enthralled.

'Shall we do that?' said one of the youths to the other.

'Or shall we go into the village and try to find him there?' that other replied. They turned their identical blue-eyed gazes full upon the still-overwhelmed Janey who remained seated on the chaise longue, her legs now folded up beneath her, staring at them in dumb entrancement. They were indeed – it could now quite clearly be seen – identical twins; their wonderful beauty made this phenomenon even more than usually startling.

'What do you think?' one of them asked her.

'We'll do whatever you think best,' said the other.

Flora watched as Janey struggled for composure. Not for anything would she have interrupted this scene, momentous in her daughter's life; not for almost anything would she have forgone the singular fortune of witnessing it. In a moment Janey's voice was heard, almost calm, almost collected, with a faint echo of her mother's social manner, betraying only to Flora the hint of unease and excitement to conceal which she was striving. 'Why don't you wait for a while,' she said. 'And then, if William still hasn't come back, you can go to the village.'

The beautiful youths got properly off their bicycles and

leaned them against the low wall which half surrounded the swimming pool.

'Yes, very well,' said one, 'we'll do that – shall we?' The other nodded and then stepped forward.

'I'm James Hopetoun,' he said, holding out his hand. 'And this chap is my brother John.'

Janey had now risen, and stood looking, still astonished, at their two faces. 'I'm Janey,' she said meekly. 'Janey Beaufort.'

'Janey,' they said, together. 'How do you do?' She shrugged very slightly and then at last managed to smile.

At this moment the disregarded Nell – who had been sitting some distance away and watching the whole scene with gleeful interest – looked up at Flora's window; catching sight of her mother she sank her head as far down as it could go between her shoulders and grinned deliriously, putting a hand over her mouth for further emphasis. God forbid that she should give Flora's presence away! Flora put her finger silently to her lips and Nell, comprehending the injunction, ceased her grimacing and turned her gaze back to the group. The twins had by now engaged Janey in suitable chit-chat: was she too staying here – had she been here long – did she like it? 'Oh, *yes*,' said Janey. 'It's *pukkah*.' The twins both laughed; one now glanced enquiringly across at the wide-eyed Nell, and Janey, following his glance, came a little to her senses. 'That's my sister Nell,' she said. 'Nell: these are some friends of William's.'

'I know,' said Nell. 'I've been listening.' The twins laughed again; Nell jumped into the pool and started to swim nonchalantly around, so showing them of how little account they were, and Janey – self-possession evidently growing, if slowly – invited them to sit down, which they did.

'Would you like something to drink?' she asked; and they having assented, she made her escape.

Flora met her in the kitchen. 'I see we have visitors,' she said. 'Who are they?'

'Oh, just some friends of William's,' said Janey.

'Ah,' said Flora. 'Schoolfriends, I suppose.' Janey shot her a look.

'Oh, hardly,' she said. But of course, as transpired later, they were. It was while Janey – with some assistance from Flora – was getting their drinks that the Hunters all returned from the village; the twins were invited to stay for lunch, informed the whole party that they had cycled the five kilometres or so from their own *gîte* (where their parents expected their return *before nightfall*) on the chance that William might care to come on an excursion with them that afternoon – had he a cycle here? – and, further, informed everyone that *their* village would be *en fête* on the following Sunday, and that it might be worth the while of William, and anyone else who cared to, to show up there and see the fun. 'Yes, *I'll* come,' said William enthusiastically. '*Absolutely.*'

Janey sat, dumbly looking down at her plate; Flora's heart almost bled for her, while William and his friends began to negotiate the time and place of their meeting, with much topographical data from the twins' side and much calculation about the length and time of the journey by bicycle from William's. Flora, glancing at Janey's hanging head, could have wept, but suddenly John – or was it James? – looked across at the silent girl. 'What about Janey,' he said. 'Wouldn't you like to come?'

Janey's head lifted, as if on a spring, and she stared at him. 'I can't,' she said tragically. 'There's only one bike.'

As Flora sat wondering whether or not it could be

opportune to offer to provide transport, Nell entered the fray. She had been listening with some avidity to the twins' and William's plans but the inclusion of Janey was signal enough for her. 'Can we go too, Mum?' she said. Her plea was echoed with fevered urgency, first by Denzil and then by Thomas: all three, ignorant as they might be of the nature of the entertainment on offer, were now determined to partake of it. The consequence was that the entire household undertook to be present at the *fête*: but it was clear to Flora that once there Janey would do all that lay in her power to detach herself from the other members and make a fourth with the heretofore despised William and his schoolfellows.

Her behaviour with William now at last became what it ought in Flora's view always to have been: she was modest, pleasant, obliging and friendly; she had been chastened; such is the power of Eros. Beneath all this modest, pleasant, obliging friendliness, Flora detected as Sunday approached a growing anxiety bordering on panic which issued in the frantic cry that she had nothing to wear: but Flora succeeded after some argument in demonstrating that this was not the case; and after a great deal of trying on and casting off, both of her own wardrobe and of Flora's, Janey managed at last to put together an ensemble that she felt would pass muster. 'After all, darling,' said Flora, lying on the bed watching her, 'who is going to see you? Only a couple of dorks. Although, I must admit, they've got awfully long eyelashes – I don't know whether you noticed, did you? – for dorks.'

15

Simon was too busy to go in for extra-marital love affairs, even if he'd believed them to be permissible. He hadn't in fact considered seriously the question of whether they were, or were not, permissible; there had been no reason to do so, for it had never arisen.

Of course, if Simon had had an ideological bias towards, or a natural proclivity for, extra-marital love affairs, it might have been another matter: he might have found the time, somehow – in the way that a lot of men even busier than he did. (Women, too, come to that.) Simon, if you'd asked him, would probably have said, after all, I have to direct such a lot of it I don't have any libido left for the real thing, ha ha.

All the same, a lot of men (and women, too, come to that) would have found – did indeed find – that directing sex scenes only increased their libido. But it didn't take Simon that way. Simon just got on with his work, efficiently, on time and within budget, and then went home to Flora and the kids.

And Flora might be looking a bit seedy, as was to be expected after three children and so on, but he *loved* her, whatever that might mean – not that Simon could have told you, precisely, what it did in fact mean. Who can? He hadn't given the question any conscious or prolonged thought; he had not needed to; it had not arisen.

David Packard was a television writer – author, indeed, of more than one of those sex scenes which Simon in his time had directed and it was his partner Sarah Frame, an actress (although not now conceivably in sex scenes) who coming across Simon in the canteen one lunch-time had taken pity on his bachelor state and invited him to dinner at the Packard–Frame establishment in Camden Town. 'Dave'd love to see you I know,' she said. 'He's working on a new six-part series.' 'Oh yes?' said Simon. 'Sounds great.' 'You haven't even heard about it yet,' said Sarah. 'No, nor have I,' Simon agreed. 'But it sounds just great.' 'Well, let's see, how about Friday?' said Sarah. 'Great,' said Simon. He didn't want to go at all, but how could one refuse these well-meant invitations? So on the Friday night which marked almost exactly the halfway point in his family's absence from home Simon found himself looking for a parking space in the vicinity of Camden Square. He was driving the little Fiat because Flora had taken, naturally, the big car.

It was Sarah who opened the door to him. 'Come through,' she said. 'We're in the kitchen.' So he followed her down the narrow passageway to the back of the house, where there was a big overdressed kitchen, and there, sitting at the wooden table in its centre, was a woman he didn't know, hadn't foreseen, couldn't have expected, here or indeed anywhere else, a woman whom Sarah – as if this were still the mundane world where such things naturally follow – introduced to him as Gillian Selkirk. 'Gillian,' repeated Simon. 'How do you do?' And she simply smiled.

16

Simon had forgotten what this felt like, this bolt from the blue. One does. He stood there, feeling weak at the knees and stupid, wanting both to remain and to flee; impaled. 'Well now!' said Sarah, 'what will you drink? Some of this?' There was a bottle of wine opened on the table; Sarah got him a glass. 'Why don't you sit down here for the moment,' she said. 'Dave will be back in a tick.' Simon sat down awkwardly – his knees still weak – on a chair diagonally opposite Gillian Selkirk, and sipped at the wine. It wasn't awfully nice. Gillian Selkirk caught his eye and smiled very faintly and Simon smiled back and looked down into his glass and sipped again. Sarah was busy at the stove. 'So, Simon,' she said, 'how's it going?' They talked shop very briefly and then Sarah brought Gillian Selkirk into the picture.

'Gillian here's an accountant,' she said. 'She's been looking into one of these dodgy Lloyd's syndicates.'

'Ah,' said Simon. He was speechless.

'Naturally, she refuses to tell us anything about it,' Sarah went on. 'I dare say it's over our heads anyway.'

Simon found his voice. 'Sure to be,' he said.

'Oh, I hardly think so,' said Gillian. She had one of those dark mezzo-soprano voices, the colour of mahogany. 'There's no mystery about accounting, it's perfectly straight-forward.' She was wearing a little black linen dress with a white collar and a pair of wildly expensive-looking shoes, and she had rather straight flaxen hair, which might have been artificially coloured, because her eyebrows and eyelashes were darker, and her eyes were hazel-brown.

'Anyway, she's been giving Dave a few pointers,' Sarah went on, 'for this series he's writing: it's about the whole Lloyd's thing. But fictionalised, obviously.'

'I see,' said Simon. He looked across at Gillian Selkirk. 'That's awfully good of you,' he said.

'Oh, well,' she replied, 'we City types will grab any chance to mingle with the artistic set. It does such wonders for one's credibility in the Square Mile.' Simon wondered how that blighter David Packard had managed to snaffle this particular accountant. His heart was still pounding uncomfortably; looking into his glass he saw that despite the poor quality of the contents it was now empty.

Sarah read his thoughts. 'Our accountant – Georgie Bligh – he's yours too, isn't he, Simon? Dear Georgie looks after us all – put Dave in touch with Gillian.'

'I owed Georgie a small favour, anyway,' offered Gillian. 'He sorted my mother out.'

'Useful man,' said Simon.

'It would take more than an accountant, more even than Georgie, to sort my mother out,' said Sarah. She picked up the wine bottle, which was now empty. 'Oh, silly me,' she said. 'We've been drinking the cooking wine. Well, let's move on to something better, shall we?' She took a bottle of something different from the refrigerator and began to open it. 'I wish Dave would show up,' she said.

'Here, let me do that,' offered Simon; and he drew the cork. Then David came in, and it was time to eat, so the dinner which was to compensate so fully for Simon's misfortune in having been detained in London while his family were on holiday in France began. Would that it never had.

17

As far as David Packard was concerned this was a working dinner: this was his best and even last chance to learn everything he needed to know, all the answers to the questions which had arisen after his and Gillian's first meeting, lunching with Georgie Bligh at a City restaurant where the odour of money made one slightly lightheaded, and the exquisite excellence of the food was a complete irrelevance.

She explained everything rather neatly: David's questions became more intelligent as time went on, and Simon became interested in the subject in spite of himself. 'Think you'd like to have a crack at directing this thing, old cock?' said David.

'I'll see when you've actually finished writing it,' said Simon.

'Work of a moment,' said David.

Simon thought, in a moment of something near panic, or shame, of his own still inchoate project. He should be in Hammersmith, working on it – or at any rate, towards it – not sitting here in Camden Town opposite a woman called Gillian Selkirk from whom he couldn't without difficulty take his eyes. It was almost, now, towards the end of the meal, as if she too had become aware of this fact and was holding the other end of a line which he had thrown to her. At moments it might seem slack, at others taut, but never did she seem altogether to let go. Simon began to be afraid.

'The question is,' said David, 'is it a scam, or is it a cock-up? That's the question.'

'Yes,' said Gillian. 'That is indeed the question.'

'Or is it,' said David – after all, he was a writer, he got *paid* to think these thoughts – 'is it a hellish hybrid of the two? I say, that's not bad, is it? *Hellish hybrid.* What do you think?'

'Well, there's the alliteration, there are always marks for that,' said Sarah. 'But I'm not really happy about the coupling of the Anglo-Saxon word with the Greek. Not really. That seems to work only when it's done for comic effect.'

'Wonderful woman,' said David to the others, 'isn't she? Read English, you see. Knows all these things.'

Simon looked at Gillian, he dared to look at Gillian. 'Is he right? Is it – for want of a better phrase! – a hellish hybrid?' She smiled at him, returning his look. 'It's too soon to say,' she said. 'And so it may be for a long, long time.'

'Just like life, really,' said Sarah cheerfully. 'Shall we have some coffee?'

18

'Could I just ring for a cab?' said Gillian.

'Oh, look,' said Simon, 'I can give you a lift. Where do you live?'

'Oh, that would be awfully good of you,' she replied. 'Bayswater, actually. But look, not if it's out of your way, really.'

'No,' said Simon, 'not a bit. Not at all. Truly.'

'It isn't,' said Sarah. 'Simon lives in Hammersmith.'

'Oh, I see,' said Gillian. 'Well, in that case – '

So here they were, getting into the tiny car. 'My other car's a Volvo,' said Simon. 'Estate.'

'Naturally,' said Gillian Selkirk lightly.

They drove in silence all the way to Bayswater, through the streaming Friday night traffic: Simon did not dare to speak, and she seemed not to wish, or to need to. She was painfully close: he could have reached out and put a hand on her knee so easily that it was extremely difficult not to. As they approached Queensway she gave him some directions and after following them he found himself outside a block of mansion flats. 'Here we are,' she said. 'Home sweet home.' There was something ironical in her tone. Did anyone else live there? Was she expected – with anxiety, with longing? 'My cat will be starving,' she said.

'Ah,' he replied. 'Poor puss.'

She unfastened her seat belt. 'Well, thanks so much,' she said.

'My pleasure,' said Simon. Dear God, was this absolutely all? Suddenly she leaned over and – just perceptibly – kissed his cheek.

'Why don't you give me a ring sometime?' she said.

Simon was stunned. Had this really happened? He sat there like an idiot watching her cross the pavement and put the key in the lock. As she unfastened it she turned slightly and briefly waved to him and then she pushed open the door and vanished. Simon still sat, staring at the closing door, the empty pavement, the rearing red-brick façade of the mansion block. Beyond the awful desire he felt for this woman – this unlikely, unforeseen, almost frightening woman – there seemed to yawn a black abyss: but why this should be so he could not begin to understand. But these things happen, he told himself; it's not as if she's the first woman I've fancied, since I became a married man. There must have been countless others. And I can't now remember even one of them.

But he could have done, if he'd tried. And he knew, inescapably, that none of them had affected him as this one did. Shaking off this knowledge as well as he might he drove as fast as he dared back to Hammersmith. After all, he said again to himself, these things happen. These things happen, to other people, all the time.

19

It was as if someone else were telling him what to do: as if an immaterial Other had entered his body and imposed its will, so that his hand, reaching out for the correct volume of the telephone directory, was really the hand of that Other and his eye, searching down the column of surnames, then of initials, was really the eye of that Other; and then his hand – that hand – again, picking up the receiver: all these movements seemed to take place in a dimension quite separate from his passive gaze; and now, in consequence, he heard a strange telephone bell ringing.

It was eight days since he'd first met her. It was Saturday evening; it was the hour when the drinks trays come out, when the baths are run, the babysitters are fetched, the fingernails are painted, the front-of-house staff begin to arrive, and the last of the millions of winking, twinkling, dazzling lights go on: the hour when everything is permitted. Even this.

'Hello? Oh, Gillian? This is Simon, Simon Beaufort, we met last week – '

'Yes, yes, I remember clearly.'

'Oh. Ah. Ha! Yes – well look – '

'How are you?'

'Oh, I'm well, thank you, and you?'

'I'm fine. Nice of you to call.'

'Oh – well – yes; look – I mean, come to think of it,

I've probably chosen a completely stupid time, I dare say you're doing something else – the fact is, I just wondered if you might feel like going to see a film with me tonight – there's something good on at that Whiteley's cinema, so I just thought – but as I say, you're probably on your way somewhere else already, no matter, some other time perhaps – ' No. No other time. This is it.

'No, I'm not. I'd love to. Where shall I meet you, outside the cinema?'

So it was just as simple as that. There was nothing to it, nothing. Ask and it shall be given. And so Simon began falling into the abyss, in all its black, fathomless depth.

20

'Which one do you like the best?'

'I like them both the same.'

'Yes but which one do you really, *really* like, *really.*'

'I don't like either of them, really, *really.*'

'You *do.*'

'I do *not.*'

'I *know* you do.'

'I like them the same,' Thomas piped up, 'because they *are* the same. They're *exactly* the same. That's because they're twins.'

'Yes of course they're *twins,*' said Nell, impatient at his intervention, 'that's the whole point. I only want to know which one she *likes.*'

'I don't *like* either of them,' said Janey.

'Ho, ho, ho,' said Nell. 'Pull the other one, it's got bells on.'

Flora was listening to all this through the kitchen window. 'Nell!' she called. 'Could you come here a moment? I need you.'

Nell came inside. 'Do leave poor Janey alone,' said Flora.

'Why?'

'Because I ask you to.'

'No, but why?'

'You'll understand one day.'

'You're always saying that.'

'It's true.'

'When will I understand?'

'When you're a little bit older.'

'I want to understand *now*.'

'The sentiment does you credit. But you'll just have to wait, I'm afraid.'

'I only asked which one she liked.'

'Which one what?'

'Which twin.'

'Why do you want to know?'

'So that I can tease her.'

'Why should you want to tease her?'

'It's fun.'

'It's naughty.'

Nell was silent, and looked at the floor. 'It isn't *fair*,' she said.

'What isn't?'

'Being the younger. Nothing *ever* happens to me. It isn't *fair*.'

'Oh, poor little Nell. Come here.' Flora put her arms around Nell and cuddled her. 'Poor little Nell,' she said. 'We'll have to make something happen to Nell, won't we. Would you like something nice, or something nasty?'

'Something nice,' muttered Nell.

'Well,' said Flora, 'I'll see what I can do. Are you sure you don't want something nasty?'

'Yes,' said Nell.

'Sometimes you can't have the one without the other, you see,' said Flora. 'Sometimes in that case it's better to have neither.' This gave Nell something to think about, so she was silent.

'In the meantime,' said Flora, 'what shall we do tomorrow?' They talked about the possibilities, one or two of which included the Hunters and another which didn't, and Nell generally cheered up and stopped feeling sorry for herself. 'In a few years,' said Flora, 'such a lot of things will begin to happen to you, I promise.'

'But what will I do until then?' wailed Nell.

'You could try and read more,' said Flora. 'For a start. And perhaps, when we get back to London, you might like to start going to a dancing class.' She said this off the top of her head.

'Oh, can I?' said Nell eagerly.

'Of course, if you like,' said Flora.

'Can I go to ballet?' said Nell.

'Yes, I should think so,' said Flora. 'Oh, that's *pukkah*,' said Nell.

'But you needn't tell the others yet,' said Flora. 'It can be our secret, until it's all fixed up.'

'Okay!' said Nell.

'But no more teasing,' said Flora. 'Okay?'

'Okay.'

So after this she left poor Janey alone; but it was difficult. Indeed, it was difficult.

21

'Did you like that?'

'It wasn't bad.'

'Shall we have something to eat now? Do you feel like a Chinese? There's a good one here somewhere, isn't there?'

'You must let me pay.'

'I won't hear of it.'

'Then I won't come with you.'

'We'll go halves then.'

'Like the adults we are. Good.'

When they were eating he said, do you always refuse to be paid for? and she said yes, generally speaking. 'In any relationship,' she said, 'autonomy is a primary good.'

'Oh,' said Simon.

'And it has to begin with financial autonomy,' she said. 'Even when it doesn't end there.'

'I see,' said Simon.

'Good,' she said.

She asked about his work; he said nothing about his *Grande Illusion*. 'I'm just a hack,' he said.

'Like me,' she replied.

Simon leaned back. 'How did you come to choose accountancy?' he said. She was picking up a fritter: she was the sort of person who's very good with chopsticks. She was wearing another of those simple, costly outfits: a skirt and jersey; you had to have an eye for these things before you so much as noticed. You see (they said) I don't have to try; I wouldn't even dream of it.

'Oh,' she said, 'I intended originally to go to the bar. I actually read law, but then, I thought well, sod it; it will be *years* before I'm earning enough to feed a cat. Autonomy again, you see.'

'Yes, I see,' said Simon.

'Of course, I probably won't stay forever in the private sector,' she went on. 'My plan was to earn enough to buy a decent house and perhaps a few shares, and then go into the SFO. Or the NAO. Or something of the kind. You know.'

'Yes, I see.'

'The idea of hunting down City scoundrels appeals to me greatly,' she said. 'Down these mean streets, etcetera. Or should that be, *labyrinths*. Even better. But the money's absolutely pathetic, you see.'

'Will you really be able to give it up when the time comes?'

She looked at him, astonished. 'Of course,' she said. 'As soon as I've got the house and the shares. That's my autonomy insurance, you see. Not a *lot* of shares. Not a *huge* house.'

'I see,' said Simon, again. He was almost mute with amazement. Here it was, the new woman: autonomous.

'I don't,' she said, deftly picking up a last mouthful from her plate, 'care about money *as such*.'

'Ah,' said Simon.

'I mean, do you?'

'I never thought. That is – having none – to speak of – the question hasn't arisen.'

'Need a question arise, in that sense, before one thinks about it?'

'No-o-o, no of course not.'

'Well then?'

'I suppose, if I cared about money, I'd be in a different game, wouldn't I?'

'Yes, I dare say so.' She looked away; the subject was exhausted. He felt that he had failed in some way. 'I've spent a lot of time alone,' she suddenly said – as it were, in explanation of what had gone before. Simon was jolted back from the sense of failure, of unease, to which their exchange had brought him: he looked, slightly puzzled, at her face. Her brown eyes looked out at him from its pale, almost unremarkable – almost plain – oval: nearly expressionless: almost completely candid, like those of an animal or a small child. 'I've thought about lots of questions,' she said. 'I always assume other people have too.'

'My wife's like that,' Simon said, without thinking; and then he did think, and was appalled. 'I'm sorry,' he said.

'No,' she replied. 'There's nothing to apologise for. There it is.' There was a silence: not – surprisingly – uncomfortable, but deep. It was to be endured. It was part of the deal. Simon had not truly understood, until this moment, until this realisation, that there was a deal. It was he who spoke first. 'Let's go for a bit of a walk,' he suggested, 'shall we?' She smiled at him, and began to rise. 'Excuse me a moment,' she said.

Simon signalled for the bill, and when it came punctiliously counted out his half share and half the tip, while he waited for her return. Flora and the children had been mentioned and briefly discussed, in Gillian's presence, in Camden Town. She knew as much as she ought, as she could wish: that subject was now and forever dealt with. It was the flag which waved, bravely, just beyond the edge of the abyss. No matter how far he might fall, he would never lose sight of it; neither would she; there it was.

22

Their walk brought them naturally, in due course, to her front door. 'Will you come in?' she said. He simply nodded, and followed her into the building.

Luxury, of the bathetic kind. She turned her head and grinned at him. 'Nice here, isn't it?' she said. They ascended several floors in a very opulent lift and then walked the length of a corridor, and she unlocked a heavy mahogany door. 'Here we are, then,' she said. 'Come in.'

She led him into a vast almost empty sitting room – a standard lamp was alight, and a blue chinchilla cat sat on a sofa in its glow. The curtains had not been drawn; the windows looked across the street at another mansion block opposite. She caught sight of his face. 'Oh, dear,' she said. 'I'm so sorry – I should have warned you. *Too* awful, isn't it?' She laughed. 'Sit down, anyway, and I'll get you something to drink.'

'No, really, nothing to drink,' said Simon.

'Or would you like some tea?'

'Tea would be terrific.'

Simon was still staring around the room. How could such a place be her home? It contained nothing but two very large leather and chrome sofas, with some matching arm-chairs, and a Shiraz rug; and there was a large pedestal desk by the windows with an old office chair drawn up to it. Gillian sat down next to the cat, who had not moved, and waved at the other end of the sofa. 'Do sit down,' she said, beginning to laugh again. 'Oh my dear, if you could see your face! I'll get the tea in a moment – just let me explain – ' but she continued to laugh, and Simon joined her. 'You see,' she said, 'well – it's a long story, but this flat was actually Albie's idea.'

Oh God. 'Albie?'

'Albert J. Short *the Second*. An American broker with whom I lately cohabited. He went back to the US eighteen months ago, never to return. I just haven't had time to turn this place in for something else. Well, there's not really much point, until I'm ready to turn it in for *the* place. That little grey home in the west that I was telling you about. So in the meantime – but at least I got rid of most of the Albie f and f. He had a strange penchant for Harrods furniture department, had Albie. Well, Harrods everything, actually. Dear Albie.'

'Tell me about him.'

'He jogged. That was why he insisted on buying this particular flat. So close to the park. Straight up the street, and you're off. And then there was the baseball game on Sunday. So you see – anyway.'

'And?'

'Oh, we were just a couple of crazy kids.'

'You were?'

'Pretty much. Well, I was a bit of a drip before I met Albie. Little Miss Muffet with a nice tidy game-plan. Albie taught me to dance, as it were.'

'Good for Albie.'

'Right.'

'But?'

'Oh, it came to a natural end. No, really. No tears, no recriminations. We still fax each other once in a while. He's just got married, actually. I was invited to the wedding.'

'Did you go?'

'I would have, but it was just too awkward to get away at the time. As it was, I sent a present that I knew Albie would simply *love*.'

'This is a bit disconcerting.'

'Is it? Let's have that tea then.' She left the room, and Simon sat on the leather sofa, thinking about Albert J. Short the Second, who had taught her to dance.

'And this cat,' he said, when she returned with the tea, 'was that Albie's choice too?'

'How did you guess?' she said. 'I don't even like cats! But Albie had to go to New York for a week, just after we moved in. On the Saturday morning after he left, Harrods – who else – telephoned to make sure there was someone here: they said they had a special delivery for Miss Selkirk. I was expecting something spectacular in the way of cut flowers, but half an hour later, this turned up. In the form of a kitten, you understand. In a *de luxe* cat basket, accompanied by a week's supply of cat food and the rest of the parapher-nalia. And his pedigree. So that I wouldn't be lonely, you see.'

'I hate to say this,' said Simon, 'but that Albie is beginning to sound something like a *pukkah sahib*.'

'Oh yes,' she said, smiling; 'he *was* something like. Certainly *something* like.' She stopped smiling and her expression was suddenly remote. 'Do you take sugar?' she said. 'Milk?' She gave him the cup of tea. 'But no one's perfect,' she said.

Desire for her had been waxing and waning from one hour in her presence to another; she would seem to invite, and then to elude him. Sometimes she seemed to lead him, unintentionally, into a dark cul-de-sac of the spirit where desire was quite unthinkable.

'Not until they die,' Simon said. 'Then they become perfect. Read the obituaries if you don't believe me.'

'True enough,' she said. 'Well, that's something to look forward to.'

'As long as you want to be perfect.'

'But of course I do.'

He could have sworn that she was quite serious.

'You're a funny girl,' he said.

'I'm thirty-three.'

'A *long* way from perfection.'

'I can certainly use the time.'

'You've got such a lot more than I have.'

'Not *such* a lot, surely.'

'It seems a lot to me.'

'At any rate, then, you're nearer perfection than I am.'

'All appearances to the contrary.'

He reached out to replace his empty teacup on the tray and she took it from him. Their fingers touched very briefly. They were out of the cul-de-sac. It was time. She glanced around the room. 'I really should do something about the rest of this stuff,' she said vaguely. 'Perhaps I'll send it to an auction.'

'Good idea,' he said. 'Do it soon.'

'The bedroom's alright,' she said. 'I was entirely responsible for that.'

'Ah,' he said.

'Would you like to see?' she said.

'Yes,' he replied, 'I would.'

She got up, and took his hand. 'It's this way,' she said.

23

Simon could see, driving back to Hammersmith, just before dawn, after his first night with Gillian Selkirk, that his life was going now to be quite different, in some way that he could only barely foresee. All that was certain was that he had been re-invented in some deep and fearful manner.

No sooner had he crossed the threshold of that bedroom than coloured lights had seemed to flash on and off madly in his consciousness and his veins had filled with their multi-coloured energy: her power of bewitchment had become the power to transform and even to control and he had truly found himself in a new mode of existence. What had seemed surely the descent into an abyss then appeared rather – or also, simultaneously – an ascent into an empyrean other-world. He had not waited even to undress properly or to let her do so. It had been horrifying, and glorious, all at once: the dread which he had felt from the start had become one more thing, one ultimate thing, to be embraced.

So this was where he lived, was it? This the house – this plain brick three-storey façade with its five white-framed windows, its dark blue door with a brass knocker (nice work there, Mrs Brick) – this his hallway, these his children's macs, that his wife's umbrella in the cast-iron stand? Simon went, unwillingly, to face the worst of it, into the kitchen, and sat down at the table: and after a few moments of simply sitting, waiting, bringing it all into focus, this room so redolent of

Flora and the children, he thought, who was the man who lived here before?

And he truly could not remember how it had felt, before, coming in here, in the evenings, say, after work; reaching for the gin; that life was too obscure now even to inspire a sense of loss. The question of whether this new creature I am has acted rightly or wrongly, Simon thought – but he had not thought: he had been inspired, the thought had come unbidden, like a gift of the spirit – the question is simply not pertinent. He had entered a realm beyond right and wrong. He had stepped – simply in the natural course of events, without seeking to do so – into a world where there was no need, and no place, for such questions: where one simply acted. It was a benefaction, which he had done nothing – that he knew of – to deserve; it was simply a piece of luck, beyond reason or justice. He had entered a sort of paradise – yes, that was as near as one could get to describing it. This was not a matter for either celebration or sorrow; it was a simple, neutral fact. All he had to do hereafter was to walk very carefully along the straight line before him.

He felt quite calm. If he'd been a believer – in any sense of that term – he might have thought, thanks be to God; but as he was not – in any sense of that term which he comprehended – he only thought, *there it is*. And just for an instant he heard the echo from the depths of the abyss, yawning fathomlessly on either side of this fine straight line where his feet were now planted.

24

'Why me?'

'Oh, you were the first candidate who turned up.'

'The first candidate for what, exactly?'

'For the job, obviously.'

'Which job would that be, precisely?

'What does it look like to you?'

'I wouldn't dare hazard a description.'

'Oh, *go* on.'

'No, really. You thought it up, you tell me. I'm only the successful candidate. What *exactly* is the job?'

'Fucking me stupid.'

'Is that all?'

'What more do you want?'

'Isn't it, in this context, more a question of what more *you* want?'

'I don't want anything more.'

'Truly?' He looked at her, searchingly. She looked back at him.

'I don't believe there can *be* anything more,' she said. 'Not truly.' Simon was silent. He began to caress her breast. 'How stupid do you want to be?' he murmured. 'Completely moronic,' she said. 'I'll let you know if ever I get there, okay?' 'Fine,' said Simon. And so it was. Sex, after all, is an awful lot more than it's cracked up to be.

'It's going to be more difficult after next weekend, you

realise,' he said to her later. 'Yes,' she said. 'I realise.' But he knew, and she knew, that just whenever he could, Simon would come to the mansion flat, by car or taxi or even if no other conveyance were available on foot, and they'd go on, like this, working through the near-infinity of sensations which were the integers of this cosmic frolic. It was a simple, neutral fact.

25

On the last night at the *gîte*, when the Hopetouns had all come over for supper, and they had all played charades – the twins had brought the house down, but William hadn't done too badly either: William was coming on: even Janey would have had to admit it – and Thomas had fallen fully clothed into the pool, and Denzil, also fully clothed, had jumped in after him 'to save him', and the twins' mother, 'beautiful blonde barrister' Serena, had sung a heartrending version of 'Father Come Home', and they had all agreed, to a tiny child, that this was the life, alright, in la douce France, and they were bloody *fools* not to pack it in and move down here for good, Flora said to Honoria Hunter in the kitchen after the Hopetouns had gone – 'See you in London! See you at school! See you soon!' – and while Jack was doing some preliminary loading up of the Hunter Volvo, 'You know, Honoria, for two pins I almost *would* pack it in and move down here for good. Seriously.'

Honoria was at the sink, up to her elbows; she turned around. Flora *was* serious.

'But darling how could you, really?'

'I don't know. But I do truly wish I could.'

'There's your business, for a start.'

'Don't I know it.'

'And then, think of the children's schools.'

'They'd get at least as good an education here for nothing

as the one we're paying an arm and a leg for back in the UK.'

'Yes. It's enough to make you weep, isn't it.'

Flora was almost ready actually to weep. Honoria noticed this.

'And then, what about Simon? You couldn't really expect Simon to pack it in.'

'No; I dare say not.'

'So there you are, really.'

'Yes, there I am.'

'Oh dear. It is sad leaving, isn't it.'

'It is.'

'*Douce* France.'

'Yes, *bien douce*.'

'It won't go away, you know.'

'I pray to God it won't.'

'Of course it won't. The French will see to that.'

'And if they don't, we shall.'

'You bet. If ever we spot them falling down on the job, we'll come straight over and sort them out. That's what the tunnel's for.'

'Yes, of course – I'd forgotten the tunnel.'

'So there's nothing to worry about, you see. You can come back just like that, any time.'

'Yes.'

'Pity Simon couldn't come.'

'I'm quite glad, actually, in a way.'

'Are you?'

'It was nice to be alone with the children for a while.'

'But you've often been, when he's been on location.'

'It's different, here.'

'Oh. Yes. As we were saying.'

'Especially with Janey at the awkward age.'

'Oh, that's what you call awkward, is it?'

Flora laughed. 'Horrid Janey,' she said. 'Darling William.'

'It's been such fun,' said Honoria.

'Yes,' said Flora. 'I can't remember when I was happier.' And she suddenly realised that she hadn't spoken to the Blessed Virgin even once since arriving in France: was not that remarkable? On the way home the next day, she began to pray. *Hail Mary, full of grace*, she said, *blessed art thou among women*. Stop that, Thomas. Not when I'm driving. *And blessed is the fruit of thy womb, Jesus. Etcetera.*

26

'Everything looks so terribly clean and tidy. Immaculate. As if you've hardly been here.'

'Well, Mrs Brick came on – when was it?'

'Thursday. *Days* ago.'

'Well, I haven't actually been here much – only to sleep and change, really. I've been working late. Editing.'

'Oh I see. How's it looking?'

'Okay. It will do.'

'That's good.'

'Flora – '

'Yes?'

'Oh, nothing.'

'What is it?'

'I'm sorry I couldn't come to France. I really am.'

'So am I. Never mind.'

Lies, lies. Flora might not have minded hers more but she at least was in a position to attempt a correction. 'That is,' she said, slowly, 'it's a pity, of course. But on the other hand, it might have been a blessing in disguise.'

'Oh?' Alarm, only just concealed.

'Well, I mean – you know – it's probably quite a good thing, sometimes, for me to get away with the children, just me. Without work and school and London in the way. I mean, I feel I hardly see them, sometimes. I felt so much nearer to them, down there.' And without you, too, getting in the way.

70

'Ye-e-es,' said Simon. 'I see.'

'Perhaps you should try it too, some time.'

'God are you serious?'

'You could take them camping.'

Release at last. They both laughed merrily. 'I'll give it my serious consideration,' said Simon, and they laughed some more.

'In the meantime,' said Flora, 'what have you got in for our supper?' She and the children had reached London in nice time for this repast; the children were upstairs bathing and changing and quarrelling and ringing up all their friends and watching television and generally reverting to their bad old London ways.

'Oh God,' said Simon. 'Please forgive me. Bugger all, as a matter of fact. Look, I'll take you all out.'

'Let's just phone for a pizza,' said Flora. 'We've already eaten out twice today. So it would seem have you.' She looked around at the immaculate kitchen. 'Where's that pizza number?' she said, hunting in a drawer.

Simon had begun, at last, to see her: the miasma of fear and guilt had begun to disperse. She seemed thinner, sleeker, more vital, and the sun had slightly bleached her hair. 'You're looking terribly well,' he said. She turned her head and looked at him.

'I am terribly well,' she said. '*C'est la France. La douce France.* It's a sort of elixir.'

'Yes,' said Simon. 'I know what you mean. Well, *vive la France.*'

'Anyway,' said Flora, 'here we are again. Is there any gin?'

And so they, too, reverted to their old ways, in which they were so well practised that almost nobody would have been able to detect any difference at all from the *status quo ante.* If Simon had been given to self-congratulation, as men (and women, too, come to that) occasionally are, he might have congratulated himself, but as it was he went on simply treading the fine straight line where Fortune had placed his feet: it took all his wits to keep from falling sideways irretrievably into the echoing abyss to either side of it.

27

'I say Simon old cock! Hey!'

Not as old as you might think. 'Oh – David! How goes it? What are you doing here?'

'Same as you I shouldn't wonder. Meeting a producer.'

'There's *my* producer now. Lizzie! over here!'

'Hey, that's *my* producer. Lizzie!'

'Alright we'll share her. There's just enough to go around.'

'Hello you chaps – oh, good table, well done Katrina. Katrina's my super new secretary. How are you Simon? How's Flora? David? How's Sarah? Good, good. Yes, Alf's fine too. God, let's have a drink. Lots of drinks. Simon, I asked you along just in case, but it's all still rather in the air. You understand. But this could be a biggie. Capital-B biggie. After all, the Lloyd's thing – US interest, etcetera, etcetera. All that asbestos and the rest of it. So, David, sock it to us.'

So David socked it to them.

'I'm just thinking,' said Lizzie – she never stopped – 'there might be a tie-in here with Scunthorpe.'

Both together: '*Scunthorpe?*'

'Yeah: *the Scunthorpe Literary Festival.* The agenda this year – it happens in October, right? – is an all-out confrontation with the crypto-philistines. Who aver that contemporary English writers – egregiously, *novelists* – have failed to deal with the great issues of our day. You know, *the issues.*'

'Oh yes; *those* issues.'

'Right. So the idea, as I understand it, is to have one posse demonstrating that English writers *are* dealing with the issues; and another demonstrating that it is not in fact the business of literature to *deal with issues*.'

'You get them coming and going, then?'

'It's the only way, with crypto-philistines. You've got to get them for being philistine – '

' – and then for being crypto – '

' – or else they bounce back again, thicker than ever.'

'I take it,' said David, 'that I for instance would join the first posse.'

'I was thinking,' said Lizzie, 'that you could fire off a few rounds from either one. Or both. After all – '

'I have dealt with a few issues, in my time.'

'But you're more than capable of doing without them,' said Lizzie. 'I mean, issues – '

'*Are* rather vulgar,' said David.

'But they do cut the mustard on the small screen,' said Simon.

'That's my point,' said Lizzie. 'Say you were to give Scunthorpe a little preliminary prospectus, so to speak, of your forthcoming telly series about the Lloyd's thing.'

'Dare I?'

'Such good publicity,' said Lizzie.

'I suppose you noticed,' said David very modestly, 'that my series is not so much about the Lloyd's thing *as such*, as it is about the – ah – Golden Calf.'

'The Golden Calf,' said Lizzie and Simon together.

'Yes,' said David. 'Do you know that painting, by Poussin?'

'Oh, of course,' they said together. Well, obviously *of course*. It's in the National Gallery.

'Well, that's it, really,' said David, still looking modest. 'That's what my series is really about.'

'Have you got Moses and the tablets in there?' asked Simon.

'Any day now,' said David.

'This really *could* be a biggie,' said Lizzie. 'And I think we should go to Scunthorpe. Well, I'm going anyway, actually, because I'm producing a prog about the Festival for Channel 4.'

'Busy Lizzie,' they murmured admiringly.

'So, David – if you think you could be ready willing and able to take part, say, in the big debate, which is going to be *bloody*, enemies will be made *for life* – have a think about it and let me know, and I'll have a word with Nicola and see if you can be slotted in.'

'Who's Nicola?'

'Nicola is my man in Scunthorpe.'

'Sounds rather like a woman.'

'Yes, she is, as a matter of fact.'

'As long as she thinks like a man.'

'Is there any other way? Obviously, she thinks like a man.'

'Rationally.'

'Logically.'

'Purposefully.'

'And pragmatically.'

'Isn't it nice now that we're all equal and have sorted out all our differences?'

'It's wonderful. I was saying to Sarah only the other day, I don't even notice she's technically a different sex from me any more, hardly.'

'It's funny, but I said the exact same thing to Alf just the other night.'

'The odd thing is I've absolutely never said that to Flora.'

'Didn't you even think it?'

'I don't remember doing so. Very odd.'

'You're out of touch with your thoughts.'

Simon had to think fast, very fast. Mustn't let that ping-pong ball fall off the fountain. 'It's just that I don't appreciate Flora properly,' he said. 'That must be what it is.' And to his surprise, he realised that he'd just, quite inadvertently, spoken the plain truth. *In vodka pravda.* He laughed happily. 'I suppose I should make a point of telling her some time pretty soon,' he said.

'Say it with flowers.'

'Should I?'

'Absolutely.'

'Gardenias,' said Lizzie. 'She deserves nothing less.' And she too was, as inadvertently, telling the truth: but she could not know it, and did not, therefore, laugh, happily or otherwise. 'But back to our onions,' she said; and they left the ping-pong ball to fall soundlessly into the basin of the fountain, and began to discuss with the maximum seriousness David's – and Lizzie's – and, all going well, Simon's – new project, a six-part drama series all about the Lloyd's thing. Or, rather, the Calf, *même* . A *biggie*.

28

'I've been drinking too, actually.'

'It suits you.' He began kissing her and then suddenly stopped. 'Who have you been drinking with?'

'A journo.'

'Which one?'

'Called Maclise. Alexander of that ilk.'

'Alex. Everyone calls him Alex.'

'It's Alexander on the byline.'

'Alex everywhere else.'

'What a lot you know.'

'He's a friend of ours.'

'Rather attractive, I thought.'

'Think again, or I'll kill you both. What were you doing drinking with him anyway?'

'Another favour to Georgie. Alex is writing a book about the Lloyd's thing. He wanted some dope.'

'Yes, Alex likes his dope, as I recall.'

'So he's a friend of yours. What a small world it is.'

'I tell you, London is hicksville. Everyone knows everyone, sooner or later.'

'New York is probably just the same.'

'I dare say that soon everyone in New York will know everyone in London, and vice versa.'

'That will be fun.'

'Are you sure? I'm not. The Atlantic conurbation. Horrible.'

'You must try to be more modern.'

'Personally, I blame the fax machine. Communication these days is just too damned easy.'

'I got a fax from Albie today.'

'Quite a day you've had all round. How's Albie?'

'Albie's okay. Asked after the cat.'

'Has that cat got a name?'

'Albie called him Solomon. I usually call him Puss.'

'Puss is more suitable than Solomon.'

'I think so. Nice and soft.'

'Puss. Come here, puss. No, not you, Puss, you stay where you are. You're not the one I want.'

Oh, and how he wanted. It was a sort of paradise, alright.

Later, 'It's time I buggered off,' he said.

'If you must.'

'I'll call you.'

'You do that.'

He went downstairs and into the street and flagged down a cab. Oh fuck, he thought, I should have done something about those gardenias. He'd really meant to buy Flora some gardenias: call it superstition, if you like. It had seemed like an essential thing to do: even though it hadn't been his own idea; even if it had been said as a joke. Gardenias: well. Not exactly chrysanthemums, were they? He'd see to it in the morning – that was the ticket. First thing. They'd probably have to fly them in from Hawaii. So much the better! Such was life on the fine straight line!

29

Maggie Brooke – Alison's sister-in-law, actually, not that it signifies – Flora's partner, whose children were both at boarding school, stayed at the atelier until closing time every day, bless her, so that Flora could get away in time to pick up the two younger children from their schools. Janey could get herself home, but she was strictly forbidden to loiter. She had a key, in case she got home first; Flora didn't like it, but what else could she do? She never loitered either, more than the traffic dictated. Janey didn't mind, but she always jumped up when she heard the Fiat, and opened the front door to them. And then said casually, Oh, hello Mummy, and indifferently lifted her cheek to be kissed, while Nell and Thomas rushed past her into the house, shrieking.

But today she stood at the top of the steps, crying 'Hey, Mum! There's a box here for you!'

And Flora said, 'A box? What sort of a box?' A *box*?

'I don't know,' said Janey. 'It's in the fridge. Mrs Brick left it there with a note.'

A box, in the fridge. 'Goodness,' said Flora. 'Let's go and see.'

She opened the refrigerator and there, indeed, was a box. 'Dear Mrs Beaufort, this box come for you today p.m. Have put it here on account perishble being flours. Yours, M. Brick.'

Flora looked at the name on the box. 'Ooh la la,' she said.

Nell and Thomas had by now received the vibrations of mystery and excitement and were gathered to witness the revelation. 'Open it, Mum,' said Thomas.

'You know,' said Flora, 'I do believe I will.' And she did.

A velvet-thick fragrance rose in great white plumes, suffusing their souls with an ecstasy almost unbearable – and yet never quite sufficient: like an ambrosia the desire for which grows with the drinking thereof.

'Oh!' cried Nell.

'Ah!' cried Janey.

'Oh, what *is* it?' said Thomas.

'I think I must be dreaming,' said Flora.

Gardenias; gardenias, in the plural. Several of them, nestled creamily together in a ravishing little bouquet, surrounded by their green leaves and tied with a pale green satin ribbon. 'Oh!' said Flora, gingerly picking up the box and smelling the flowers from close to. 'I can hardly bear it.'

'Let us smell too,' the children cried.

'But be very careful,' said Flora; 'you must never touch gardenias, or they go brown. Thomas, can I trust you? Very *very* careful, darling.' The children very carefully smelt the flowers.

'Oh, it's blissful,' said Nell.

'It's *pukkah!*' said Thomas.

'Who sent them?' said Janey. Flora picked up the card.

'I wonder,' she said, and smiled. 'Don't ever leave me . . .' it said, '. . . for a day longer than a month. S.'

'Who sent them?' said Nell.

'Just a chap I know.'

'Who?'

'Can't you guess?'

'Not Dad,' said Janey. 'Not *Dad*.'

'Why not?'

'Not Da-ad,' said Nell. She and Janey were both giggling. 'Not *Dad*,' they cried, dancing about and shrieking. 'Not Dad!' cried Thomas, mystified altogether, but determined to join the party. 'Not *him*!' They didn't get over it for days; not until the gardenias had turned — as, alas, they must — quite brown, and were all (except one) thrown away. Nell got the piece of ribbon, because she asked for it first, but Thomas got the box. Janey, of course, was too old to care about that sort of thing.

30

It wasn't going to be quite so easy from now on, at least for a time.

'Poor darling, you look knackered.'

'You know, to tell you the plain truth, I *am* knackered.'

'This is the first time this week that you've come in before midnight. The children haven't seen you to speak of for days.'

'You know the form, Flora.'

'Is it nearly finished?'

'Yep. Nearly finished. No more late nights.' What the hell was he going to do? There was some barbed wire across the fine straight line, to be stepped over very very carefully, leaving no tell-tale scratches.

'Louisa wondered if we might dine next Friday, can I say yes?'

'Sure. Say yes.' Why not.

That was the least of it. He'd been sleeping in the dressing room since Flora's return from France – he usually did that anyway when he was working late; she was a nervy sleeper. It was time to return to the deep peace of the marriage bed: but actually it was peaceful no longer: it was the place above all others where he was bound to see (if only to glimpse) that there did exist the question of right and wrong. It might not truly be pertinent: he might inhabit a sort of paradise beyond its writ: but in that place, where Flora was so near to him –

near to him spiritually even more overwhelmingly than she was physically – he couldn't but see that there remained, theoretically, such a question. That it could, theoretically, be pondered, by another if not by him. That he could, theoretically, be convicted as a malefactor. By Flora, for example. This was a piece of barbed wire which would take a lot of stepping over.

Flora was stitching: tapestry seat-covers for the dining room chairs. She would tell you laughingly that she expected to complete the last one by the year 2000. No, not flowers: seashells. A different kind for each chair. The scallop, the conch, the nautilus . . . resting on the sand, with the wide ocean's wild depths in the background; and sometimes a cloud or two in the sky above. 'Flora, you are clever!' '*And* industrious.' 'It's terribly good therapy, actually.' She stuck her needle in the side of the canvas and rolled it up. 'Shall we go to bed?' she said. 'Let's just have a nightcap first,' said Simon.

He rose from his semi-supine sprawl and fetched the bottle of Armagnac which Flora had brought back from France. 'Just a very tiny one,' she said. He handed it to her and she sipped carefully. 'A thimble full of the warm south,' she said. He laughed, and took a much larger mouthful. He smacked his lips. 'These frogs are so bloody clever sometimes that they leave the rest of us standing,' he said. 'But we had the Empire,' Flora pointed out.

'They had an empire too.'

'We had *the* Empire.'

'Yes, it's true, isn't it? Pretty amazing, really.'

'Dreadful, of course.'

'Oh yes, *dreadful*. Never live it down.'

'But pretty fabulous, all the same.'

'Yes, that's it. Literally, metaphorically, fabulous. You

missed some amazing cricket while you were in France, by the way.'

'Not quite. William and his friends kept track on the World Service and then regaled us in some detail.'

Simon laughed. 'One thing the frogs didn't think of,' he said happily. 'Couldn't have thought of. Not them. Not in a zillion years.'

'Not the cucumber sandwiches *either*,' Flora said.

'We're alright really, aren't we?'

'Yes, we're alright *really*.'

'Shall we go up?'

Flora put down her glass. 'Yes,' she said.

Simon climbed into bed beside her: he had showered; his hair was still damp. He put his arms around Flora. She smelt of verbena. The barbed wire was behind him. 'I love you,' he said. It was true.

3 1

'Do you love me?'

'Do I *what?*'

'Love me.'

'Good God. You know how I feel about you.'

'Do I?'

'If you don't then you haven't been here. I've been fucking a ghost, all these weeks. Here, ask the cat. Ask Solomon. How do I feel about your mistress, Puss?' The cat sat quite still, staring at them steadily. 'You heard him,' Simon said. He sat up and helped himself to one of her cigarettes. 'Love,' he said. 'You want love, too, do you?'

'I didn't say so.'

'Then why did you ask?'

'Simply out of interest.'

'Your interest was frivolous, then.'

'Gosh, sorry. I didn't realise that I was expected always to be serious.'

'About some things, yes. As you'd expect me to be.'

'You're being very masterful this evening.'

'You've provoked me into it. Perhaps that was your intention.'

She thought for a while. 'No,' she said. 'I really wanted to know what you think of me. As a person. Sort of thing.'

'It was my understanding that you wanted to be fucked

stupid, and nothing more. In fact I think you said that there can *be* nothing more.'

'It's true that I don't believe that people can give each other anything more – not without setting up some sort of horrible dependency; and then good-bye autonomy. Of course. But that doesn't mean that one has no impression of the other person, of their character, their personality, their moral worth, etcetera. I mean, you must know me quite well by now – don't you?'

'The concept of knowing, in the sense you've just used it, is pretty much beyond my comprehension,' said Simon. 'I don't claim to know you in the way you suggest. Our relationship is quite rigidly defined. It would otherwise be out of the question. We're lovers, that's all. There's nothing more to it.'

'You wouldn't care, if anything happened to me?'

'I'd regret it bitterly and even at length. You're the fuck of a lifetime. As you very well know. As you even intended you should be – I mean, that *is* the game, isn't it? Not chess, not tennis, not roses round the door and 2.4 children, but pure unadulterated sex. Of course I don't want anything to happen to you.'

'Until you've done with me.'

'Or you with me.'

They were silent. 'Now that you've raised the matter,' said Simon, 'I suppose I'm bound to ask you, whether you really are quite sure that this is all you want. If not, all that there ever can be.'

'It's a question of what is really possible,' she said, 'within the limits of maintaining one's autonomy.'

'This autonomy,' said Simon.

'I saw what the lack of it did to my mother,' she said.

'You may find yourself having to think again,' said Simon.

'Sooner or later. Don't you really want ever to marry? Well, if not actually marry, at any rate commit yourself to a full-time all-out relationship? To say nothing of having children.'

'Not so far,' said Gillian Selkirk. 'Right now I've got other fish to fry.'

'Fair enough,' said Simon. He had caught a glimpse of the flaw in her perfect, impregnable notion of autonomy and of the personal frailty which it had been designed to protect: but he did not want to ponder these things now. If ever. 'The trouble is,' he said, 'I just haven't got the time, the way things are, to fuck you *really* stupid. If I had, you wouldn't be asking all these questions.' He put out the cigarette and turned towards her. He reached out a hand and began to caress her. 'Why me?' he said. 'Considering the disadvantages.'

'I just fancied you,' she said. 'A lot.' So there they were.

He was managing to see her now only two or three times a week, and then not for very long, but as he drove back to Hammersmith he thought, well at any rate there isn't much chance as things are of our getting bored with each other. They hadn't even arrived at the stage of getting used to each other.

Not that he'd ever become bored – exactly – with Flora. But that was utterly different. All those years. All those children. And all the rest of it. Mother of God. As Flora would say.

32

'I'm just going for a walk.'

'Why?'

'I just want to.'

'Let me come with you then.'

'No, you stay with the children. That's the whole point. See, you don't even have to get up. You can stay here with the papers, all you have to do is listen out and make sure they don't kill or injure each other.'

'Can't Janey do that?'

'No, Janey's one of the children.'

'Oh God, alright then. Off you go. Why are you wearing that lot?' It was her tweed suit, with the nice fitted jacket.

'I just want to. See you soon. Bye-bye!'

Why was she going for a walk, in a suit, on a Sunday morning?

Oh – ye gods! Simon leaped out of bed and ran to the window. 'Flora!' he called. She was at the bottom of the path already; she turned and waved and then kept on going. 'Come back soon!' he cried, but it was a pretty hopeless effort. It was too late to do anything. Much too late to stop her. But he knew – oh, he knew what was afoot: he'd sussed it, just a moment too late: Flora was going to church. He should have seen it coming.

He got back into bed with the papers, but it wasn't the same any more, so he got up and showered and dressed.

He'd glanced at the time just after his *éclaircissement*: 10.45: right, so now, he was thinking, she should fetch up again around 12.30: ish. And then he had a rather brilliant idea. He looked at his watch, and laid his plans.

At midday, 'Come on, you kids!' he called. 'We're going for a walk!'

Nell's face appeared around the bannister at the half-landing. 'Why?' she said. 'And where's Mum?'

'You'll find out,' said Simon, 'if you come for a walk with me.'

'I don't want to go for walk,' she said.

It took some doing. Even rounding them all up took some doing: cajoling them – ordering them – enticing them – bribing them – that, basically, was what it came to – took some doing. Ye gods, kids! They were beyond belief.

Simon had learned one or two useful things, if not *the* useful thing, during his summertime walks around Hammersmith: *viz*, that there was a Roman Catholic church some considerable distance away, and two Anglican ditto nearer to hand, one Low, one High. (You could tell by reading the notice-boards, if not otherwise.) And Simon's money was on the last of these. He'd heard about these lapsed Romans: they often – even generally – used the Anglican church as a sort of halfway house on the way back. Sometimes they stopped right there. And why not? Good enough for Dr Johnson, wasn't it? Simon led the children forth, and bent their steps towards the High Anglican church. So what the hell, if Flora wasn't there he could give them a brief lecture on the Gothic revival and then march them home again. They trailed along in his wake, protesting the while.

'Where are we going?'

'Why can't we take the car?'

'What if Mum comes back before we do?'

'What if she doesn't have her key?'

'What if I don't take you to Alton Towers at half-term?' said Simon. That shut them up.

You could hear the organ thundering, and the congregation singing, as they approached the church. Stirring stuff, these C of E hymns. What would Flora be making of that lot? It would probably tip the balance. Oh, God.

This at any rate must be the last piece of the business within. Simon and the children were standing around under a yew tree, and the children were asking him what they were going to do now. 'Wait,' said Simon, 'just a minute.' The organ delivered one last rodomontade and a silence fell which lasted for several minutes. Then suddenly the organ began again, more exuberantly still. Ah: the procession. Not long now.

And, sure enough, here came the priest, divested of his major finery, in an alb. 'Look,' said Thomas. 'That man is wearing a dress!'

The priest stood at the doorway, greeting his exiting congregation. How sweet it all was, honestly. Simon really had to agree. Yes, it was harmless after all – the barmy old C of E – and it was *sweet*. Part of the heritage, wasn't it? Should get a grant from the DoE, or the English Tourist Board, or someone. Or hand it all over to the National Trust to look after. Whatever. Good God, there was Flora.

33

Simon, the only one of them all who was not entirely astonished at the encounter, stood aside from their squeals and exclamations, grinning happily. Flora, the younger children's curiosity satisfied (Janey's could not be articulated, at least for the time being), at last met his eye. 'Funny we should run into you like this,' he said.

'Yes. Of all the gin-joints, in all the towns, in all the world – '

'I thought we might all go out to lunch. Ages since we've done that.'

'Where can we go?'

'There's that new place down by the river. All you can eat, and a jazz band.'

'Oh! are you sure? That would be *smashing*.'

'Come on then. Come on kids, we're on the move again.'

'Oh dear, look at them. Do you think they're fit to be seen in a place like that? Nell, your *hair*.' Flora began trying to tidy Nell's hair. 'And Thomas, do pull your socks up.'

'They'll do, don't fuss, they'll do. This isn't France.'

'No,' said Flora, looking around. 'You can tell at a glance.'

She felt so happy, so unutterably happy, sitting at a big table in the restaurant with Simon and the children, drinking Chablis, eating chicken pilaff, and salad, and toffee pudding, and everyone else having just what they fancied, having helped themselves from the buffet (Thomas had sausages, and sausages: 'You said I could have what I liked! I don't *like* salad and vegetables!'). She felt, sitting there with the family all around her – all out together for the first time for several months, wasn't it? – so unutterably happy that she couldn't imagine whence came that dark shadow that fell on her sometimes, filling her with an awful, aching dread; she could hardly remember how it felt, that awful dread. It was just something silly. It was just, she supposed, that she loved them so very much. Love was something which grew with time. The more you did it the deeper it became. It was natural, she supposed, to fear for the people one loved, and for whom one was responsible. That was all. Here she was, as lucky as a woman could be – oh, how lucky. She mustn't be afraid. 'Perfect love casteth out fear.' Oh, how beautiful, how very beautiful. Now to see if it were true. Now to see if she couldn't make it true. Perfect love. Not another kind. She caught Janey's eye.

'How's my Janey?'

'I'm okay.'

'Have you had enough to eat?'

'Yes thank you.'

'Simon, you couldn't get me some coffee could you?'

'Dad, can we go and see the boats?'

'I'll take them. I'll just get your mother some coffee first. You both wait there. Does Janey want coffee?'

So she was left alone with Janey.

'Are you alright, darling?'

'Yes.'

'Good.'

'Mummy?'

'Yes?'

'Why did you go to church today?'

'I just wanted to see what it was like.'

92

'But why today?'

'I dunno. One just has these impulses, you know.'

Janey accepted this. 'What was it like?' she said.

'Rather nice, actually.'

'In what way, nice?'

'Well – nice. I can't tell you. It's one of those things you have to find out for yourself.'

'Are you going to go again?'

'I might. I'll see.'

'I can't see why you'd want to go to church. You don't believe in God.'

'No, that's true. But then I don't not believe, either.'

Janey was confused. 'You could come too if you wanted,' said Flora. 'And see what you think of it all.'

'I don't know,' said Janey. 'I mean, I don't believe in God.'

'Well, you're only thirteen,' said Flora. 'You haven't had that long to think it over.'

Janey sat there. 'I quite liked that organ,' she said.

'Oh yes,' Flora agreed. 'The organ's pretty hot stuff. Even better inside.'

'I might come, one day,' said Janey. 'Or I might not.'

'That's the ticket,' said Flora. 'Can't say fairer than that.' Janey pulled a face at her and they both laughed. 'Do you want to go out and see the boats?' Flora asked.

'No,' said Janey; 'not unless you do.'

'We'll stay here, then,' said Flora, 'and be nice and cosy. What if you get us some more coffee?' So Janey did. I've got to find some way of spending more time with her alone, Flora thought. She's at that age. I could lose her confidence. It would kill me.

34

Simon was staring out of the window, wine glass in hand. 'I might give David a call,' he said. 'See how he's getting on.' Flora, sitting at the kitchen table, said nothing. The children were all in the sitting room watching *Our Hospitality* on video. 'But then,' Simon went on, 'one doesn't want to look *too* enthusiastic, at this stage.'

'You're enthusiastic then, are you?' said Flora.

'Ish,' said Simon. Then he turned around and gestured vaguely with the hand which was holding the wine glass. 'Talking of enthusiasm,' he said.

'I wondered when you might get around to that,' said Flora.

'Yes, well. I mean – what?'

'I shouldn't worry, if I were you.'

'You're quite sure about that?'

'It was only an Anglican church, after all. I recall I had your permission for that.'

'Humph. Permission. Look – '

'I wonder what you think this is all about, that it should vex you at all.'

'If I knew what it was *about*, it wouldn't *vex* me.'

'Come along and find out, and then you won't *be* vexed.'

Simon ignored this enticement. 'And that isn't the half of it,' he said. 'What *actually* vexes me is the thought that this may be only step one of the journey back to Rome.'

'Rome,' said Flora, ruminatively.

'Yes, *Rome*.'

'You make it sound a pretty dire destination,' said Flora.

'So it is,' said Simon unhesitatingly.

Flora laughed. 'You Protestants have such ideas of the place,' she said.

'The facts speak for themselves,' said Simon. 'Glossing over them is the most pernicious form of sentimentality, to say no worse.'

'That could be so,' agreed Flora mildly.

'Anyway, by the way, I am not *a Protestant*,' said Simon. 'I am not an anything, as you know, other than a rational creature.'

'Oh, yes, of course,' said Flora.

'Don't humour me. I'm serious.'

'Alright,' said Flora. 'Well, as to your being rational, I can only say that I am not entirely confident that you have considered all the data, and a conclusion derived – however rationally – from an insufficiency of data is not in the end a rational conclusion.'

'What if I don't admit some of your so-called data to be anything other than fanciful suppositions, or even illusions?'

'Then surely you would have to discountenance the Church of England as deeply as you do that of Rome.'

'No,' said Simon. 'The doctrine of the Church of England is minimal, and was always – *and rightly* – intended to be; that of Rome is notoriously and wilfully extravagant. The degree of delusion in the first case is harmless and in the second dangerous.'

'Anglicans seem to believe all sorts of different things,' murmured Flora.

'That which they all believe,' said Simon, 'could be written on half a sheet of A4.'

'Well, I'll see what I think,' said Flora, 'after I've given them a fair trial.'

'God,' said Simon. 'Are you saying that you actually intend to make a habit of this churchgoing, then?'

'I might,' said Flora. 'I'll see how I feel. I'll see how I get on.'

Simon poured some more wine. 'What was it like?' he said. 'First impressions.'

'Oh, very nice,' said Flora. 'Nice *is* the word.'

'Yes,' said Simon. 'Niceness is, after all, the English – and *a fortiori*, therefore, the Anglican – speciality. It's only a question of determining what the word really means.'

'It's not nearly as simple as it looks.'

'That's the English for you. So it was nice, was it?'

'And more. Perhaps.'

'Did you actually commune?'

'No.'

There was a silence. Simon was too tired, for the moment, to go into all *that*. 'Oh, *Flora*,' he said.

'Oh, *Simon*.'

He drank some more wine. 'I thought you were happy,' he said; and then immediately wished he had not.

'I am happy,' said Flora. 'Mostly. I mean, how could I not be? I'm one of the fortunate of the earth. We both are. We all are. Of course I'm happy: as happy, that is, as it's possible to be, in the world. It's just that that happiness is – well – '

'Yes, I know it's transitory,' said Simon; 'obviously. But that is the whole point of it. As of everything. To substitute for a true awareness of this essential transience a belief in an illusory God-the-Father and all that pertains thereto seems to me a retrograde step.'

'God-the-Father,' said Flora. 'Well, perhaps belief – in some sense – in God – in some sense – is the only way of arriving at a true awareness, as you put it, of the essential transience. For some of us, anyway.'

They were silent. 'I would hate to lose you,' said Simon – he, the adulterer – in a low voice. 'My life would be sour grapes and ashes.' Flora laughed: the quotation came from one of their favourite authors. But Simon sat unsmiling, staring at the table, overcome for the time being with a sense of what it might be to have 'lost' Flora, and her laughter died away.

'It looks to me,' she said, 'as if your transience-awareness could use a bit of heightening.' A more dreadful awareness was dawning on Simon at this moment: that of his own apparent duplicity. The fine straight line was a narrow path, alright. Just when you thought it could get no finer, it did.

'That must be true,' he said; 'yes.' He drank some more wine, and Flora got up and started the supper. Soup, she thought; I'll get some vegetables into Thomas.

35

Lydia and Louisa were eating salt-beef sandwiches in a place on the edge of Soho, which was handy for Louisa who worked backstage in a famous shop in Regent Street.

'Fabulous,' said Louisa.

'Brilliant,' said Lydia.

They munched for a while and Lydia wiped her mouth. She looked around at the lunch-hour crowd – the usual West End potpourri. 'Lunching,' she said. 'I must do a series on London lunching some time, for Floating World.'

'Terrific,' said Louisa. 'Do it.'

'It's only a question of time, and money.'

'Strange how many questions boil down to those two things,' said Louisa. 'I've noticed it frequently.'

'Yes, most,' said Lydia. 'I say, Louisa?'

'Yes?'

'A really funny coincidence happened to me the other day.'

'Tell me about it.'

'I'm walking along Westbourne Grove, okay?'

'Okay so far.'

'Because I've been to see one of my photographers – he lives in one of those funny squares to the south of, okay?'

'Still okay; go on.'

'And I see this Volvo coming along, so that makes me think of Flora, you know.'

'Yes, Volvos make me think of Flora too.'

'It's silly really because after all Claire and Alex, for example, have a Volvo too.'

'But with them it's not quite the same, somehow.'

'They're not so Volvo-*ish*.'

'Actually I suppose we'd have a Volvo too if we had another child, but as it is, with only Fergus we can just about get away with the Peugeot.'

'Would that be a good reason for not having another child?'

'It's probably one.'

'Well, be that as it may, Flora pre-eminently has a Volvo, and the children to put in it, so when I see a Volvo I think of Flora.'

'Which you must therefore do quite frequently, no?'

'Exactly. *Exactly*. So there I was, this day – early evening actually – seeing a Volvo and thinking of Flora for the zillionth time, on the streets of London, except that this time, who do you think was actually driving said Volvo?'

'Flora, of course.'

'No, Simon.'

'Well, same thing.'

'Yes but don't you think that's a huge coincidence?'

Louisa thought. 'Yes, it is,' she said. 'When you think of all the Volvos there are, driving about.'

'Exactly.'

'Did he see you?'

'No. He looked pretty preoccupied, actually.'

'Kids in the car?'

'No, it was empty.'

'I wonder,' said Louisa, 'what Simon was doing in Westbourne Grove.'

'Travelling westwards,' said Lydia.

'Hmmm,' said Louisa. 'Not exactly his stamping ground, I would have thought. Oh well.'

'None of our business.'

'No, none whatsoever.'

Lydia laughed. 'Women really *are* different from men,' she said. 'I don't care what anyone says. They ask more questions.'

'Different ones, at any rate,' said Louisa.

'*Vive la différence!*'

'*D'accord.*'

'I say, Louisa.'

'Yes darling?'

'I saw an awfully nice handbag in your shop just now, before I came here. Just what I'm looking for.'

'Okay, show me the one you want and I'll get it for you.'

'You are a dear. Do you still get the same discount?' 'Yes, still the same.' Lydia calculated. 'I'll give you a blank cheque up front,' she said, opening her wretched old handbag, 'and you can fill it in later, okay?' 'No problem,' said Louisa. 'Shall we go?' And they tripped happily back together to the famous shop in Regent Street.

36

'Ooh, lovely handbag Lydia, is it new?'

'Brand new. Louisa got it for me at her discount.'

'Even then.'

'Yes, even then.'

'Business must be good!'

'Well, *ish*, I wouldn't say more.'

'But ish is good!'

The waiter came and they ordered. Last week salt beef in Soho, this week fettuccine in the Fulham Road, thought Lydia. Life is a lunch. She looked around. Yes, she must do that series. Lunching in London. London lunching. London at lunch. 'What do you think?' she asked Flora. Flora knew her words. All too soon they were overcome by the absurdity of the words lunch, luncheon, lunching, and had to abandon the matter for the time being. 'It'll come to me,' said Lydia. 'Suddenly. In a flash.'

'That's right,' said Flora.

'How's Simon?'

'Simon's okay.'

Suddenly, in a flash, Lydia forsook her intention of telling Flora about the funny coincidence of two weeks ago, when she'd seen Simon travelling westwards along Westbourne Grove in the family Volvo.

'That's good,' she simply said. 'And how are the children?'

Flora told her. 'I didn't know what I was letting myself in

for,' she said. She was telling Lydia about Nell's dancing lessons. 'We got there, on the day,' she said, 'and Thomas was with us, of course, because we'd gone straight from school, and Thomas took one look at the set-up, saw *little boys* all kitted out and taking part, and insisted that he wanted dancing lessons too. I ask you!'

Lydia laughed. 'So I had to do the whole routine again,' Flora went on. 'Back to Freed's, tights, shoes, the lot. Of course, I don't know how long it will last. He may lose interest within a few weeks.'

'Or on the other hand he may be a principal at the Royal Ballet in say twenty years' time,' said Lydia. 'Or somewhere. It could go either way.'

'Yes,' said Flora. 'Silly, isn't it?' They both laughed. 'In the meantime,' said Flora, 'I'm run ragged.'

Lydia looked at her. 'You don't *look* ragged,' she said. It wasn't quite a lie.

Flora looked up. 'I haven't any *time*,' she said. 'I never, never have a moment to sit quite still doing fuck-all. One needs a few moments every day, well at least every other day, to sit quite still doing fuck-all.'

'Yes, I know,' said Lydia. 'I do a lot of that.'

'How I envy you,' said Flora.

'In my next life,' said Lydia, 'I'm going to have three children. I've asked for that specially.'

'Do you want the husband as well? Or just the children on their own?'

'Oh, I suppose so,' said Lydia. 'Yes, I suppose the husband as well.'

'Then do as much fuck-alling this time round as you possibly can,' said Flora. 'It's your last chance.'

37

'What are you doing?'

'Fuck-all.'

'Oh. Right. Why not. One day you're going to church, another you're doing fuck-all: I don't know what's come over you lately, Flora.'

'I'm just growing and developing as a person.'

'Oh, jolly good. Carry on.'

'You should try it too.'

'I have done.'

'Then it shouldn't surprise you when I do it too.'

'No, alright, alright. Do you want to come and see a film?'

Flora sat up. 'A film?' she said.

'Yes, a film. There's a mustn't-miss on at the Gate.'

Flora lay back on the sofa again. 'I'm sorry,' she said, 'but I must miss.'

'Go on,' said Simon.

'Anyway, there are the children.'

'Oh, Janey can cope for just a few hours,' said Simon.

'No,' Flora replied. 'Honestly. I'd truly rather stay here, and go on doing fuck-all.'

'Alright,' said Simon. 'I'll go by myself. Do you mind?' 'No,' Flora assured him. 'Not at all. Enjoy yourself,' 'It's my work,' said Simon.

'Of course,' said Flora. 'Of course it is.' Of course it was.

'I'm meant to be at the cinema.'

'You are at the cinema.'

'Some movie this is.'

'Actually, I've been wondering when you were going to turn up here with a camcorder.'

'Oh, that's what you want, is it?'

'Not especially.'

'I wouldn't have said we'd reached that stage yet, would you?' He wondered if they ever would: was there world enough and time? They had at least reached *a* stage.

'Come out with me.'

'Where?'

'Just out. Just locally.'

'Why?'

'I just want to be with you in an anonymous crowd.'

'So long as it's anonymous.'

'That's one thing about Bayswater. It's the heartland of anonymity.'

'I like that!'

'Well it is. I mean, only an American stockbroker would think of actually living here.'

'You'd be surprised.'

'Not I. Come on, let's go out somewhere. What about that new brasserie?'

'Alright.'

They got dressed. 'Will you have time to come back here again afterwards?' said Gillian.

Simon looked at his watch. 'Not tonight,' he said. 'Next time. We'll come back afterwards next time.'

In the brasserie he saw how right he was. It was intensely

exciting to sit here, in a public place, with this intensely desirable woman, knowing that one could have her later on: it would be even more intensely exciting if one knew that one should. He took her hand. 'I'm crazy for you,' he told her.

'That's good,' she replied.

'Is it?'

'Yes. It is. As good as a thing can be.'

'As good as gold?'

'Yes, exactly. As good as gold.'

38

The two younger children were already asleep; Flora was in Janey's room, glancing over Janey's homework. Everything seemed to be in order. So it had better be. Janey came in from the bathroom and got into bed and Flora switched off the light and sat on the edge of Janey's bed. 'How many miles to Babylon?' she said.

'Oh – about two thousand – would it be?' said Janey. 'Two thousand *and ten.*'

'Can I get there by candlelight?'

'Yes, and back again.'

'Perhaps we'll go there next year, then, and skip France.'

'Where's Daddy?'

'He went to the cinema.'

'When will he come home?'

'Oh, fairly soon, I expect.'

'Is he going to go away on location again?'

'I expect so, one of these days.'

'No, but soon?'

'I shouldn't think so.'

'That's good.'

'You don't mind him going away, do you?'

'Don't you?'

'Well, yes – but it's his work, after all. One just accepts it.'

'I'd rather he stayed here.'

'Perhaps he will, for a while.'

'I hope so.'

'We can manage without him, can't we?'

Silence.

'Can't we?'

'I suppose so. Not for good though.'

'Oh of course not for good. But we needn't worry about *for good*. It's only ever for a little while.'

Silence again.

'What's bothering my girl?'

'Nothing.'

'Sure?'

'Yes.'

'Positive? Truly?'

'Yes, truly.'

'Tell me if you change your mind, won't you?'

'Yes. But I won't.'

'Time you went to sleep, darling.'

'Good-night Mummy.'

'Good-night my angel. God bless.'

Flora went downstairs and got out her needlework, and went on stitching the sea. She had covered several leagues by the time she glanced at the clock and saw that it was already eleven o'clock. It must be a rather long film, she thought. She sat and stitched, waiting to hear the sound of Simon's car approaching the house, coming to a stop outside: in vain; the long minutes accumulated. At last she put aside her work and went upstairs to bed: but as she crossed the hallway, something made her quietly open the front door and stare out into the empty street. She stood on the threshold, uncertain, listening, perhaps, for a distant sound of Simon's approach. Then she shook herself. How very silly, she thought. She retreated into the house and closed the door and ascended the stairs; she looked in on the sleeping children and then went to bed herself. How was it possible – for it was of all things unreasonable – to feel so apprehensive, so desolate? God, she thought, oh God. God, she said, oh God. There was no one else to ask.

39

'What do you think of it?'

'It's good.'

Flora was reading David's just-completed script. She kept her place and looked up. 'Are you quite definitely going to do it?' she said.

'It looks like it. I'm seeing Emily tomorrow.'

Emily was Simon's agent.

'So far as I've got,' said Flora, 'it seems all to take place in London and the home counties.'

'Yes,' said Simon. 'that's it, more or less. The rest can be mocked up.'

'No long trips away then,' said Flora.

'No, none.'

'That's good.'

'I'm glad you think so.'

'Of course I do.'

'That's good.'

'I'm glad you think so.'

'Of course I do.'

'That's good.'

'Is there any gin?'

Simon went to make the drinks and Flora went on reading. When he returned she said, 'There's a little boy in here for a minute or two.'

'Yes; I thought we might use Thomas.'

'I don't want him to miss any school.'

'Well, we'll see. Here, drink this.' He handed her a glass and sat down. 'How are you, Flora?' he said. 'Is everything okay?'

Flora was sitting on the sofa with her feet up; Simon was perched on the remaining twelve inches' width. Flora moved her feet to give him more room and swallowed some of her drink. 'I'm fine,' she said. 'Everything's fine.'

'How's business, for example?'

'Oh, fine. We're getting a mench in *World of Interiors* next month.'

'Oh, jolly good.'

'It could be our big break.'

'Well done.' Simon thought about how valiantly Flora worked, and how brave she was. He was filled with a sort of anguished pity for her. He put his drink down, and took hold of one of her ankles.

'Flora,' he said.

'Yes?'

'I – I wish you were – I do wish I could make you happy.'

'That's as much as I could possibly ask.'

'Let me know if there's anything, anything at all, I can do, won't you?'

'Alright. Can you stick around on Sunday? Lydia's coming to luncheon.'

'Oh *cripes*.'

'You did ask.'

'Snookered. Fucking snookered.'

'*C'est la vie.*'

'Too sodding right.'

'She won't stay long. She's just picking up some curtain material I put aside for her.'

'I might have to go out in the afternoon.'

'Fancy that.'

'If I do take this thing on we're going to have to go like the clappers.'

'Naturally.'

'Seriously,' said Simon. Flora saw that he was serious; very serious.

'You really actually want to do this one, don't you?' she said, surprised.

'Yes, I really do, actually. I think I can make something of it. I think it's my chance to do something really good.'

'Something you believe in?'

'Yes.'

There was a brief silence. Then, 'So to speak,' said Simon.

'Oh, to be sure. *So to speak.*'

'After all – '

'Quite.'

Flora took Simon's hand. 'I love you,' she said, in a tiny voice.

He leaned over and kissed her neck. 'Darling Flora,' he murmured.

Nell came into the room. 'What are you doing?' she said.

'Nothing.'

'Can we have dinner now?'

'Any minute,' said Flora. 'Any minute now. You can set the table if you like. And then call the others.' Nell went away. Flora still had Simon's hand. 'Please don't go out anywhere tonight,' she said.

'No of course not.'

'How was that film?'

Simon had seen it several months before at a special screening. 'It was alright,' he said. 'But not what I'd call compulsory viewing.'

'That's good,' said Flora. 'I'd hate to have missed anything compulsory.'

If only she hadn't mentioned the film. But he'd given his word, now. 'No,' he said. 'You haven't missed anything you shouldn't.' After dinner he picked up the script and looked through it for a while and then he began to tell Flora what he'd been thinking about the look of the thing; the way it ought to be done; the meaning. 'It's *noir*,' he said. They talked about that, and he managed, almost, to forget about Gillian Selkirk and the invisible line – like an electronic signal – which connected them, day and night.

40

Once Tom – no surnames, no pack drill – and Terry – *a fortiori* – were well away, the thing simply took off. Blood on the floor wasn't in it. Some wag passed a whistle up to Mark – same *caveat* – who was doing his usual valiant chairing job; the dear man came in due course as close as dammit to actually using it. Other participants – David, for example – gave the topic their two pennies' worth, but in the end you had to call it the Tom and Terry show: nothing so violent had been seen on our screens (so to speak) since Tom and Jerry.

As literary festivals went, Scunthorpe had an edge, alright. A lacerating, lethal-in-certain-cases edge. Nicola Gatling, assistant to the Director, spent the afternoon succeeding the debate ministering to the walking wounded, while the Director himself saw to those requiring intensive care: as Claire Maclise observed in her summing-up as presenter of Lizzie Ainsworth's Channel 4 prog, it all showed how very much people really care about literature: and that had to be good, hadn't it?

'Sorry I missed it,' said Simon to David after the latter's return.

'Rather glad I did,' said Flora.

'Catch it on the box,' said David. 'Tape it.'

'Drink up,' said Simon, pouring more wine into Sarah's glass; 'this is tax-deductible.' He was buying them all dinner in a fashionable restaurant, to celebrate the signing of the contracts. 'It's a works outing.' He poured more wine for Flora. She looked lovely tonight, the way she sometimes still did, in a shot-taffeta suit with a fitted jacket and very full skirt. Perhaps he should simply take her out more. Yes, that was the idea. Take her out. They could go to the ballet, for instance; etcetera. 'Our Thomas is learning to dance,' he told David and Sarah. 'What do you think of that?'

'It was his own idea,' Flora told them.

'Oh, in that case,' said David.

'I think it's lovely,' said Sarah. 'I love men who can dance.'

David and Simon talked about the great project before them, which was going to put them indelibly on the map. You had to be indelibly there by a certain stage of your career or else that career was basically *finito*. Phew, they'd just managed it. Simon wasn't stupid. He knew there was plenty of room ahead for screwing up. This festival of self-congratulation was the opener for months of hard graft. Ah, that narrow path; that black abyss: going home in the taxi with Flora he felt it all around him. By the time they ascended the steps to the front door he was stone-cold sober. They sent the baby-sitter home in the taxi and went up to bed, and he made love very silently and at length to his beloved, his brave, his lovely, his pitiable wife.

41

'Is this really all you want?'

'How could it not be? What else is there?'

'Love, cohabitation, marriage, children, companionship, shared experiences, holidays.'

'Washing up.'

'All that.'

'What if I were to say yes – to all that?'

'Do you?'

'I asked first. What if I were?'

'I suppose we'd be in trouble, wouldn't we?'

'Exactly. I'm surprised at your not leaving well alone.'

'But do you?'

'I'm not in the habit of wanting things I can't have.'

'I shouldn't have thought there's anything very much you couldn't have, if you decided you wanted it.'

'You don't actually like me much, do you?'

'What an extraordinary thing to say.'

'Alright, let's suppose I do want more: let's suppose I do want love, cohabitation, washing up and the rest of it. What are you going to do?'

'It's a nice question. But since you don't – '

'We're supposing I do.'

'Should we?'

'It was you who started this line of enquiry, not I.'

'True.'

'I wonder why you did.'

'Just wondering.'

'You wanted to make quite sure.'

'Perhaps.'

'Out of concern for me, of course.'

Simon looked at her. Had he any concern for her? Who was she, anyway? 'Partly that,' he said.

'But for the rest – ' she said.

'I'm concerned chiefly for myself,' he said. 'And mine.' She said nothing; she was thinking. 'That is as it must be,' he said. 'That is as you've always known it must be. I don't want – I can't have – complications.'

'Complications,' she echoed.

'You know what I mean.'

'Love.'

'Etcetera.'

'Perhaps you'd like to stop seeing me,' she said.

'Don't say that.'

'I'm absolutely serious.'

'Don't even think it. Don't even breathe it. You are completely essential to me.'

'Such as I am?'

'Fuck you, Gillian. Don't play games with me. Autonomy, remember? This is what we are. This is what we do. It's enough. More than enough. A whole world; and ours alone. Okay?'

He looked at her. She stared back at him. 'Go on then,' she said. 'Do it.'

42

'Why are you getting up so early? It's Sunday. Oh God, you're going to church again, aren't you?'

'As a matter of fact I'm not. And actually it isn't all that early.'

'It is. Why are you getting up? Stay here.'

'I've got to make a pudding.'

'What kind? Why?'

'Bread-and-butter. Lydia's coming to lunch, remember.'

'Oh *God*.'

'Go back to sleep.'

'You know, I think I will. Wake me when she's gone.'

'I'll wake you at eleven; you'll just have time to make yourself presentable.' Flora went into the bathroom and closed the door on her irritable husband. This was the sort of thing from which one sometimes yearned for a break – not just a few snatched hours, but a proper respite of billowing weeks. She let the shower rain down her back for a good ten minutes, and sprayed on masses of scent afterwards. She looked at her face in the mirror. I'm dying, she thought. She stared at her face, at the face of someone who had begun to die. It was not death itself she feared: not even judgement – supposing there should actually be a judgement – itself. She feared lack of preparation; shoddy preparation; incorrect preparation. She had to get it right – never mind, for the moment, why or to what end. She had to be right.

Elle se devait d'avoir raison. She knew that the alternative was a living death worse than the dying one. That was why she did not fear death itself.

She got dressed in an old frock and a cardigan and went downstairs to make the pudding: the children came in and assured her with loud cries that they detested bread-and-butter pudding, and would not, could not, eat it: why couldn't they have castle puddings instead? 'Why, indeed?' said Flora. 'It's one of the great mysteries. If you can tell me the answer I'll give you sixpence.'

'Sixpence!' they cried. 'Sixpence! What's sixpence?'

'It's what I used to get from the tooth fairy,' said Flora, 'when I was a little girl.' And she told them stories of her little-girlhood. They liked to hear these: they were tickled to death at the idea that she had once been a little girl. Not Janey, though. Janey was in the sitting room looking through the papers. Well, chiefly the colour supplements. But still. Janey was growing up. Childhood was streaming away from her in long glittering shreds; there was barely a glint of it left for the naked eye to see. 'Janey,' she called, 'come in here and help me a moment could you?' And Janey came in, and read out to her a piece about the Scunthorpe Literary Festival, featuring such household names as David Packard and Claire Maclise. There was even a photograph.

'Yikes,' said Janey. 'I didn't know Claire was famous, or David.'

'You just have to be looking in the right place,' said Flora. Fame was another thing to be dreaded, another thing which could crush you to death; but she did not tell the children this, because it seemed too terrible a thing for them to know.

43

'I might go for a bit of a drive-around,' said Simon, 'and suss out a few ideas for locations.'

'Oh good,' said Flora; 'you could drop Lydia off on the way – do you mind?'

'No problem.'

'Perhaps the children would like to go along.'

'Not this time. Truly. I can't get anything sorted with them nagging at me for ice-creams and lavatories and God knows what-all.'

'Can I have an ice-cream?' said Thomas.

'See what I mean?' said Simon.

'If only you hadn't mentioned the word,' said Flora.

'Please,' said Thomas. Oh dear.

Lydia sat smoking a cigarette and observing this scene of everyday family life: it was at once exotic and banal. 'Let me have one of your cigarettes,' Flora said to her.

'Really, Flora,' Simon protested. 'Now I've seen the lot.' The sooner he got this depraved spinster out of the house, the better. Curtain material, forsooth. He looked at his watch. 'We ought to go fairly soon,' he said. 'Or the light will go before I get a chance to see anything.'

'Ready when you are,' said Lydia equably. Flora put the cigarette out, not half smoked. 'It's not really your style, my love,' said Lydia kindly.

'No,' said Flora. 'I seem to be incorrigibly clean-living. Awful, isn't it?'

'It's just your karma,' said Lydia. 'Not your fault.'

'If your karma isn't your *fault*,' said Simon, 'I don't know what is. I thought that was the whole point.'

'It depends who you think *you* actually *are*,' said Lydia.

'Ah,' said Simon.

'What's your karma?' said Thomas.

'Oh, God,' said Simon; 'look what you've started.'

'Sorry,' said Lydia. 'Sorry, sorry.'

'What's karma?' said Nell. 'Why are you sorry?'

'Oh dear,' said Lydia.

'It's time we were off, anyway,' said Simon.

Lydia got up. '*Lovely* lunch,' she told Flora. 'Thanks so very much. And for the material – it's brilliant. I'm so grateful.'

'What's karma?' said Nell.

'Come and help me load the dishwasher,' said Flora, 'and I'll tell you.' They all said good-bye to Lydia – Janey had already gone out for the afternoon with her friend Amaryllis – and she and Simon drove off, Flora and the children waving from the doorway. Then they went into the kitchen and Flora told them, very briefly, about karma. 'This is what Hindus and Buddhists believe,' she said. 'But as you're not Hindus or Buddhists you needn't.'

'What are we?' said Nell.

'Christians,' said Flora. 'More or less.'

'She's more,' said Thomas, 'and I'm less, because she's bigger.'

'That's about it,' said Flora. 'More or less.'

44

'Still in the same place?' said Simon.

'Yeah,' said Lydia. 'Still the same.' She gave him directions again.

'Oh, yes,' said Simon; 'I remember.' The battered street, the arrested decay. When they turned into it, it was no more. Feeble saplings had become almost-substantial trees; there was fresh paint, there were window-boxes. 'I say,' said Simon. 'What's been going on here?'

'Urban renewal,' said Lydia drily. 'And so on. Sales of freeholds. New brooms. Gentrification. Progress.'

'Lucky old you.' said Simon.

'I bought at the right time,' said Lydia.

'Good for you,' he said. 'Shall I give you a hand with that?'

'I can manage,' said Lydia. 'Thanks all the same.' As she crossed the pavement to the front door, he thought, she doesn't like me, does she? Not that I care. Not that I like her all that much, come to that. If at all. She turned and waved and then went inside. She's got a nice smile, though, he thought. Too bad she never found herself a bloke. Poor old Lydia.

Simon is such a pig, thought Lydia as she went up the stairs. So arrogant. Attractive, sure, but – he just seems to take Flora so entirely for granted. Does he know just how hard she has to scramble to keep that show on the road?

What a life. Still, the children are beautiful. That is her reward. But as for Simon – oh well. There's pretty well always something wrong with a man, isn't there?

She let herself into her flat and, putting the big parcel of curtain material down, went over to the windows and started taking down the tattered old curtains.

All the other shabby accoutrements had already been banished to skips and salerooms – she'd got a surprising price for the sideboard, described by the auctioneers as a credenza: enough to re-furnish the whole room and paint it too. One of her photographers had helped with the painting, for a small consideration. The room was now virtually empty: there was a leather and chrome sofa coming up at a sale in a fortnight's time which she had her eye on – two such sofas, in fact, but they were listed as separate lots – and she might see if there were any other likely pieces when she went to the viewing.

She draped the new material, a plain off-white calico, over the curtain rails, just to get the idea. Yes, the room would look rather good. Quite the thing. Jolly nice. The only furniture it contained right now was an old deck-chair, so she sat down on it and made a spliff and had a nice quiet smoke. Life is just the saddest thing there is, she thought. Sad beyond all comprehending. Let's have some music, for God's sake. Yes, precisely.

45

'Good God, what's been happening here?'

'As you see, entrance of two strong men and exit of same bearing sofas, chairs, etcetera. Gone to the saleroom, every one. Going under the hammer in two weeks' time.'

'This is all rather sudden.'

'Not really. I contacted the auctioneers a while back but the humpers took their time collecting the goods – they came yesterday.'

The room was now completely empty, except for the Shiraz rug. He glanced into the dining room. That was empty too. 'What do you sit on?' he said.

Gillian looked down at the rug. 'I'm thinking of taking up meditation,' she said. 'I really might as well. Perhaps I already have.'

'As long as you haven't sold the bed,' he said.

'No.'

'Let's go and lie on it, then,' he said, 'before you do.' He picked her up and carried her into the bedroom and undressed her. He looked down at her while he undressed himself. 'I'm so glad I found you in,' he said. He gave one of his better performances: one of his best. He wanted to tell her he loved her. It was true. Saying so was unthinkable. He stroked the side of her face, along the hairline, thinking, I love you, I love you. She turned her head and looked at him, as if she'd heard him, out of her brown eyes, as candid, almost, as those of a child. She mustn't say, I love you: not to him. That was a thing she must never say.

'Let's go to that brasserie,' he said. It was their place. They would not see anyone they knew in there: they were safe in that brasserie. It was a nice place, too. A nice place to take your girl. They walked there through the dusk. 'Winter's almost here,' he said. 'I've never seen you in the winter.' He ordered their drinks and held her hand. 'Are you alright?' he said.

'Yes.'

The drinks came. He drank. 'That's better,' he said. He'd have to be careful. How long since the wine at lunch-time? If you led two lives you could end up drinking twice as much. Fucking twice – twice? – as much, and drinking twice as much. Holy smoke. *He'd have to be careful.*

'Are you going to buy some more furniture?' The mansion flat was now more than ever tomb-like: he'd been glad to get out of it.

'I don't believe I'll bother, for the moment.'

'Oh?'

'I'm thinking of sticking my neck out for a house I've seen.'

'Oh yes?'

'Quite nearby, actually. A few streets away.'

'Ah. Staying in the parish, then.'

'Yes. I'll show it to you if you've got time.'

'I haven't quite. Not today. Next time.'

'Alright.'

'Meet me here on Tuesday evening – can you do that? Around six?'

'I could just manage six-thirty.'

'And then you can show me.'

'Okay.'

It was a tasty little house, alright: in a nice quiet narrow little street running northwards from the Bayswater Road. 'It isn't cheap,' she said, 'but it's just what the doctor ordered. I really might as well go for it. In fact, I've put in an offer.'

'Well,' he said, 'I hope you get it. It looks okay, I must say. Have you had a survey done?'

'Everything's hunky-dory,' she said. 'It's as good as it looks.' It was, as it happened, the property – *pro tem.* – of a Lloyd's name who'd been properly – or, improperly – screwed; but she knew this only by accident; and she didn't tell him.

'And the interior?' he said.

'Immaculate,' she replied.

'Talking of which,' he said; and he took her hand and led her away, towards the mansion block, and the bedroom, and the bed. Time went so fast, so fucking fast. He was going to miss Thomas, but if the traffic wasn't too bad he'd get back just in time to see Nell; and Janey, of course. His dinner would be in the oven, keeping warm. Flora was well used to that. Pity about Thomas. But there it was. Something, once in a while, had to give.

46

Flora dropped Nell and Thomas off at their dancing class and then she didn't go home until it was time to fetch them, she didn't even go to Sainsbury's, she drove to the church, thinking she could just go in, and sit there.

It was locked, of course. Well, what could you expect? There is evil in the world: thoughtless, casual evil, and conscious, deliberate evil. Which is worse? Flora sat down on a wooden bench just outside the church porch in the cold grey afternoon, and tried not to hear the traffic, and watched the leaves falling. She supposed she might as well go to Sainsbury's after all. It had come to that.

'Hello there! Were you – ah – did you want anything?'

She looked up. The vicar. She smiled. 'No,' she said. 'It's alright.'

'We have to keep it locked when there's no one around. You know how it is.'

'Yes, of course.'

'I'll be saying mass at six o'clock, of course.'

'I'm afraid I can't stay – I have to fetch my children.'

'Oh yes. I think I saw you here, didn't I – several Sundays ago?'

'Yes, that's right.'

A silence. He was considering the situation. 'I do hope we'll see you again one of these Sundays, then,' he said. 'Or whenever. There's a low mass every weekday of course.

Meanwhile – shall I sit down here for a moment? Would you mind?'

'No, not at all, please do.'

'You live nearby, I take it?'

'Yes, quite near.' She told him the name of the street. He considered.

'I believe you're just outside the parish,' he said.

'Oh dear,' said Flora. 'Shall I go?' He laughed. Then he introduced himself, and shook hands; and Flora gave him her name, and agreed that he should call her Flora rather than Mrs Beaufort.

'Well, Flora,' he said, 'I could go and get the key, if you wanted to go inside: shall I do that?'

'It's alright, really.'

'If you're quite sure.'

'Yes, truly.'

'Is everything alright?'

She thought. He had a way, this clergyman. She was going to talk to him. 'Mostly,' she said.

'There's always a margin, isn't there,' he said.

'It's just that – I've got this feeling – somehow – that something is wrong; and I don't know what it is.'

'Ah.'

'I feel that I *must* find it out.'

'Yes, I'm sure you must. Of course, it could be a delusion. One does have those.'

'That would be the thing then that was wrong – the having a delusion. That might be worse than the alternative.'

He considered this. 'The question is,' he said, 'how to find out.'

'Quite.'

'God, being by definition omniscient, knows the truth. He might tell you. Do you believe in God?'

Flora thought. It was a matter of choosing one's words. 'In a manner of speaking,' she said.

'It's all, really, a manner of speaking, if you like.'

'Isn't there anything more than what we can say?'

He laughed. '*I'm* bound to think so, but then that's my job,' he said. 'Not to say, my *raison d'être*.'

Flora thought some more. 'What do you think I should do?' she said.

'To the end of discovering what's wrong, you mean?'

'Yes.'

'Come to church. Come and pray with us. Receive the sacrament. Have you been confirmed?'

'I'm a lapsed Catholic.'

'Ah. A Roman.'

'Yes.'

'I dare say you realise that we lot are not considered by your church to be the real right thing.'

'It isn't my church.'

'As long as you know the form.'

'Yes.'

'We for our part are more than happy to see you here as a communicant or not as you choose, whenever you wish, as I hope you realise.'

'Do you really think that this is the way to discover truth?'

'I know no other. Not in such cases as yours, at least as you've described it.'

'I wonder.'

'You could try it.'

'I could.'

'*I* would.'

'I'll see.'

'Go on. Be radical.'

She laughed. 'I don't believe I've ever talked to an

Anglican priest before,' she said. 'Apart from the formalities, when I married – my husband isn't a Catholic, we married in an Anglican church, because I was lapsed by then.' She looked pensive.

'Ah,' he said. 'Well, I suppose you've heard – I mean, it's universally known – we're all utter idiots. Don't say you hadn't been warned.' She laughed. 'Come and hear a few more of my sermons and you'll see just how true it is,' he said.

'Or how untrue,' she replied.

'Well, there is always that possibility,' he agreed, 'logically, at any rate.'

'I'll try and come on Sunday.'

'That's the ticket.'

'I ought to be going. Thank you for everything.'

'See you soon, then, I trust, Flora. God bless you.' He turned and waved and was gone.

He went into the vicarage where his wife had the tea ready. 'Whatever kept you, Freddy?' she said. 'This lot will be stewed.'

'Sorry, Phoebes. I've been about my Father's business. Encouraging a strayed lamb back into the fold.'

'Oh, jolly good, jolly good.' She poured out the tea.

'Yes. Do you remember that woman you remarked about a month ago, in the good tweeds?'

'An English rose, slightly faded?'

'That's the one. Shouldn't entirely surprise me if we were to see her again. Might even become a regular.'

'Oh, I do hope so. She looked to me as if she'd be likely to come up with some absolutely *first-rate* jumble.'

47

Simon was on edge; he had been conferring about the casting most of the afternoon.

The casting was crucial, of course. If he could get Michael *and* Nathaniel, he'd be in business. But it looked a bit tricky. If he couldn't get both, did he want either, or did he want to start again? Because his idea, his great idea, was – supposing he could get Nathaniel *and* Michael – to cast each of them against type. Because everyone was pretty used to seeing Nathaniel playing the cad (he looked like a cad) and Michael the sweetie (he looked such a sweetie). So he wanted to cast Nathaniel as the sweetie and Michael as the cad. They'd be devastating. And then if he could get – but it was a matter of hanging in there for the time being to see if he could get both Michael *and* Nathaniel. Please, *please* God. So Simon was on edge.

She was wearing a pink silk kimono with a design of black and white flying cranes; Solomon was stretched out on the Shiraz rug. There was a tray beside him with two champagne glasses and a bottle of Krug. She sat down again on the rug and began untwisting the wire. 'Make yourself comfortable,' she said.

'What are we celebrating?'

She could hear the edge in his voice. She looked up. 'Life,' she said. 'Life, liberty and the pursuit of property. My offer's been accepted.'

'Oh, *congratulations*,' said Simon. The edge had left his voice; he squatted down and then sat; he began to enter the spirit of the thing. 'Well done, my darling.' My darling. My darling. Was she wearing anything under that kimono? She drew the cork and poured out the champagne and they drank. He smiled at her. 'Tell me all about it,' he said. She did so.

'I can move in in a fortnight,' she said.

'Just like that,' he said. Well, it was pretty breathtaking.

She shrugged. 'There's nothing to it, really,' she said. 'I could move in in a taxi, practically.' He looked around. It could be true. 'There's only my clothes, and a few odd bits,' she said.

'Solomon,' he said.

'Yes, I'll take Solomon,' she replied, as if there could be any question about the matter. He suddenly saw that she was capable, just capable, of leaving Solomon with the porter, or whomever else might have him.

'Poor Solomon,' he said. And he meant it, too.

'Tsk,' she said.

They drank more champagne. He pushed the tray away, and made love to her, there on the rug, and didn't tell her that he loved her, because it was true. Oh God help him, it was true; not that he knew what it truly meant. It simply was the truth. But as long as he didn't say it, it remained deniable. As long as he didn't say it, it need not be, but could be, denied. Whereas if he were to say it, it would be undeniable. And it would have to be denied: sooner or later, by one or another, it would have to be denied. So he didn't say it. He must never say it. That was the fine line he trod; finer by the month, the week, the minute. 'I have to be going,' he said.

'Wait, I'm coming with you.'

'How do you mean?'

'I'm coming out with you. I just have to put some clothes on – I won't be a moment. I want to go around and look at the house again.'

'Oh, the house. What, just look? And gloat?'

'Yes.'

'What a child you are.' He laughed.

'No, I'm not. I've never bought a house before. Will you come with me?'

'I can't.' But he did. He stood there for a moment in the dark street in front of the house, holding her hand, looking up at the neat façade with its long windows. He squeezed her hand. 'I have to run,' he said. He bent and kissed her cheek and walked quickly up to Bayswater Road to get a taxi, and she went on looking at her house, excited, troubled, fearful, thrilled, as she had never expected to be; had never calculated upon being.

48

'Can't you manage even one evening a week? If it goes on like this – the children simply never see you. And this is before you've even begun shooting!'

'As you see, I can't. Sorry. Sorry sorry sorry sorry sorry.'

Flora said nothing. There were tears in her eyes. Oh God, God: help me. Who else could help her? 'Thomas wanted to show you his hornpipe,' she said, and she began to cry.

'For God's sake,' said Simon. Flora put her head on her arms and wept. He went over to her.

He'd forgotten how he loved her: not how much – who could measure that? – or how little; or that he did so – could that ever now be forsworn, after all these years, all these children? Only, *how*: how it was done: how it was. Something was wrong, and it might just be his fault. One false step and he might be in hell, and Flora too; and then the children. Get your act together, Beaufort.

He held her in his arms. 'What's this hornpipe?' he said. 'I don't understand.'

Flora wiped her eyes. 'You know, the hornpipe,' she said. 'The dance, the sailor's hornpipe. He's just learned it, at his ballet class.'

'Oh. I see.'

'He's really very good, you know,' she said. 'So is Nell.'

He felt more wretched still. 'I'm *sorry*, Flora,' he said. He meant it, too. 'I didn't actually think you minded being left with them. Coping by yourself. When you came back from France, you said – '

'That's different. Going away on our own is one thing. Being here together, but with you simply – a shadow – '

'Alright, alright.'

Flora's face was so sad that he could have wept himself. He got up and fetched the Armagnac. 'Let's have a hit of this,' he muttered, and poured out two glasses and gave one to Flora. He drank some of his own and looked down into the glass. 'This isn't like you,' he said. 'You were never like this before.'

She said nothing; she was staring over the rim of her glass into the middle distance. She very slightly shrugged. 'No, that's true,' she said. 'You're right. I don't know what's come over me.'

There was a silence. 'Well,' said Simon at last, 'I see I'll have to organise myself better, won't I?' Flora said nothing. How the hell was he going to manage this thing? He sat down. 'I'll make quite sure of being here at the weekends, that's all,' he said. 'I can't make promises about the weekday evenings; you know how it can go on. But at least until we start shooting, I'll keep the weekends free for the kids.' It was like a sentence; Flora perceived the similarity herself but said nothing: could say nothing: suffered, as she had for so long, the sense simply of there being something wrong which she could not identify, much less correct.

'That would be a help,' she said. 'They do need you, you know.'

'Perhaps we could all go somewhere on Saturday,' he said. 'Or Sunday. Think of somewhere you'd like to go.'

'Janey's going out on Saturday. The Hunters are going down to see William and they've asked Janey to go with them, if she likes.'

'Really? Why would Janey want to do that?'

'I truly can't imagine. Five hundred-odd youths, not all of whom are spotty – *I* can't see the attraction.'

'So she gets on with young William, does she?'

'And some of his friends.'

'Oh yes, you mean those twins.'

'I think that's the idea.'

Simon looked grave. 'They *are* growing up,' he said. 'That's a fact.'

'It's all so transitory, isn't it,' said Flora. 'Or had you forgotten?'

'Perhaps I had,' said Simon. 'Perhaps I had.' And so I have, he thought. I fucking have. Unless I've remembered only too well.

49

'Have you actually sold this place yet?'

'Albie's buying it.'

'*Albie?*'

'He's taking a position in readiness for the next UK property boom.'

'Don't tell him, but there isn't going to be one.'

'I did tell him, but he doesn't believe me.'

'Oh God, maybe he knows more than we do.'

'If he does, then the information's no good to us.'

'How true. So what, is this to be his holiday cottage?'

'He's going to let it. An interior decorator called Laetitia Crewe is about to descend, tape-measure in hand. By the time she's finished with the place it'll be worth £800 a week, give or take.'

They both laughed merrily. The thought of all that money can do that to a person.

'Still, he's got the outgoings,' said Simon.

'He won't clear much over £500 per,' said Gillian. 'The game's hardly worth the candle.' They laughed again.

'I've got something to tell you,' said Simon. This was his best chance. He told her about the weekends: about his promise.

'I see,' she said.

'I'm sorry,' said Simon.

'It doesn't matter,' she said.

What they didn't say, couldn't say, thickened all the air around them like incense.

He took her to the brasserie, not just for a few drinks but for a meal, to make it up to her, somehow, for all those pre-empted weekend hours – for the loss of those late, now lamented, afternoons snatched from the grip of the mundane. *Fonds des artichauts, grillade normande,* coffee and mints. 'Have you had enough to eat?' he asked. 'Then let's go back to Albie's.'

Later, lying on his back and looking at the bedroom ceiling, with its pointless and perfunctory mouldings, he said, I'll be glad when you've moved. And she said, so will I. And they both thought how much better, in some way now mysterious to each, it would be after she had moved into the new house.

50

He wasn't doing too badly. He could crack this thing. He might not be Father of the Year, but he'd do well enough. On Saturday he'd taken Nell and Thomas out for a McDonald's and a big screen presentation of the latest Disney; by the time he got them home he felt as if he was coming down with multiple rot – teeth, guts, brain, the lot. Except for the presence of the children themselves. The children were beautiful. Even he could see that. Being with them was like drinking the purest most sparkling spring water. It was just their taste which was abominable – in food, entertainment, toys – abominable; execrable. How could this be?

'What can it mean?' he asked Flora.

'I suppose it's simply a sign of original sin,' she said.

Janey had been delivered by the Hunters at ten o'clock, shiny-eyed. She sat on the sofa with them drinking cocoa and relating the day's events.

'And did you see the cathedral?' asked Flora.

Janey shrugged. 'Only the outside,' she said.

'She's too young for cathedrals,' said Simon. 'She's got plenty of time for cathedrals.'

'Anyway,' said Janey, 'I don't believe in God.'

'She's too young to believe in God,' said Flora. 'She's got plenty of time for God.'

'I thought the point was,' said Janey, 'I've got *no* time for cathedrals, and no time for God, much less *plenty*.'

'That's my girl,' said Flora. 'Now come and kiss me good-night, darling.' Janey kissed them and went up to bed.

'Could she be clever?' said Simon.

'I should jolly well hope so,' Flora replied. 'It's what we're paying for.'

He woke up on Sunday morning to find Thomas sitting on the dressing-table chair staring at him gravely.

'Hello,' said Thomas. 'I just wondered if you'd like to see my hornpipe again. I've put my ballet shoes on just in case. See?' He raised a small foot. Simon sat up and looked at the child. He wanted to hug him. Did one do such things? Did he?

'When I'm up and dressed,' he said. 'Where's your mama?'

'She's gone to church.'

'I see.'

'She's coming back soon.'

'Of course.'

'Janey's looking after us.'

'Excellent.'

'Will you get up now?'

'Absolutely.'

'And then I'll show you.'

And soon, soon, all this innocence would be only a shining memory. There was transience for you. From the light to the dark: and then? Could there be a path back to innocence? Could there? Was that where Flora was, now: trying to find the path back to innocence? Was that where he was: was that the destination of the fine line: or was it that line's location? He got up and showered and dressed and went downstairs to the kitchen, and Thomas danced for him again. 'That's the stuff,' said Simon. And he felt as happy as a person can ever be. Why isn't this enough? he wondered. Why do we always want some-thing more? How can this be? And he remembered his question of the day before, and the answer that Flora had given him.

51

'Goodness, tea chests.'

'A dead give-away, aren't they?'

Simon peered into the nearest one. 'I thought you said you could move in a taxi,' he said.

'It's amazing how many odds and ends you find around a place, when you get right down to it.'

'So when's the off?'

'Saturday.'

He was silent for a moment. 'Will you be able to manage?' he said.

'Of *course*. No problem.'

Well, she'd just have to, wouldn't she? It wrung his heart. She looked at his face. 'As a matter of fact,' she said, 'Jonathan said he'd give me a hand, if I needed it.'

'Who's Jonathan?'

'Oh, just a chap. Just an old mate. Jonathan Finch. We see a show together once in a while.'

'Oh, do you now?'

'You bet.'

He looked almost murderous. 'And then we have a drink or two, or some supper, and he talks to me about Nicola.'

Where had he heard that name before? Everywhere, probably; it was very popular.

'Nicola.'

'Nicola Gatling.'

Nicola Gatling. He was sure he'd heard that very name before: where?

'Nicola Gatling is the woman he loves.'

'Why doesn't he see these shows with her, then?'

'She's been working up in Scunthorpe, the last six months or so.'

Of course: Nicola Gatling: Lizzie's man in Scunthorpe. 'I know some people who've been up there recently,' he said. 'For the Literary Festival.'

'Yes, that's it. That's where the crack is, in Scunthorpe. Anyway, she'll be back in London very soon. No more shows for me then. Not with Jonathan, anyway.'

'Still, as long as he's going to give you a hand on Saturday.'

'Yes; sweet of him, isn't it?'

He was still looking pretty murderous. She stopped packing and went over to him and put her arms around his neck. 'Look at me,' she said. He looked at her. 'You don't want me to stay at home watching telly every night, weekends included, do you?' she said.

'You could play cards with Solomon, or chess.'

'Solomon isn't any good at cards or chess.'

'You could play chess with a computer.'

'But still. A girl needs a few laughs, once in a while.'

'Yes: I'm totally out of order. Disgracefully. Sorry, darling. Sorry, sorry. I – ' don't say it. *Don't ever say it.*

'Then there's Rupert.'

'Oh, is there?'

'I see the occasional show with Rupert, too.'

'Tell me about Rupert.'

'Rupert's a merchant wanker.'

'Oh, classy.'

'Right. He isn't very pretty, though, Rupert isn't.'

'You're pretty enough for the two of you.'

She lay her head on his chest. 'What shall we do now?' she said.

'I'll think of something.'

'I knew I could depend on you.'

Could she? Should she? What had happened to autonomy? Don't depend on me, he wanted to say: not for anything. Don't use the word even lightly, even in jest: especially not in jest. Many a true word. But it was too late, much too late. Some form of dependence had crept up on them, and God knew where it would end. You just had to keep going, on the long, fine, ever narrower line; God alone – that is, no one – could know where it would end. Or should.

52

'So, what, Robert will drop Fergus off in the mornings and we'll get him home – ?'

'No, well I could fetch him – '

'No, Louisa, it's too much; I'll bring him back.'

'Or Robert could – but he works so late sometimes – '

'No, look, don't worry. It's no problem. If the worse comes to the worst we'll put him in a taxi.'

'Oh yes, that's best; he loves taxis.'

Here they were again. Flora and Louisa, sorting out the forthcoming school holiday arrangements. It was a massive juggling act, every single time. Flora and Maggie had a student to hold the fort at the atelier during the school holidays, although one or other of them had to be standing by in case of emergencies, but Louisa was a full-time employee. Louisa was an executive. And Louisa had no luck with nannies, au pairs or mother's helpers. What luck she might have had was always ruined by Fergus. He had seen them off, one by one, from the age of two years onwards, until she had had to give them up altogether. So Fergus was going to stay with his grandparents in Somerset after Christmas but before that he was going to muck in with the Beauforts. Or, rather, they with him. He had a way, at eight years old, of turning a house upside-down. 'Are you sure you can cope?' said Louisa fearfully.

'It's a challenge,' said Flora stoutly. Flora was a soldier of

Christ. 'My strength is as the strength of ten,' she told Louisa, 'because my heart is pure.'

'You know, darling,' said Louisa, 'I think that's pretty true, actually.' Flora was laughing. 'I mean it,' said Louisa.

'I don't know what I'd do without Flora,' she told Robert. 'What *we'd* do, that is.'

'How do you mean?'

'She's going to mind Fergus during the pre-Christmas hols.'

'Is she, by God? Does she know what she's letting herself in for?'

'Of course she does. Fergus is notorious.'

'Really? *Notorious?*'

'Yes, *notorious.*'

'What *have* we spawned.'

'I ask myself the same question at least once a day.'

Fergus came in and they explained the arrangements to him. 'Ho hum,' said Fergus.

'What do you mean, ho hum?' said Louisa.

'Well, if it isn't one thing, it's another,' said Fergus.

'That's about the size of it,' said Robert. The rebellious look began to come on to his son's face.

'It's only for a few weeks,' said Louisa, 'after all.'

'A few weeks,' said Fergus, 'is actually quite a *long* time.'

'But then there's Christmas,' said Louisa encouragingly. 'Think about that!'

'Can I have a car?' said Fergus. Oh, dread: he'd seen some millionaire child on television driving – yes, actually driving – a scaled-down six-litre Bentley.

'Not *just* yet,' said Robert. 'Not until we've got our own private road. But we'll think of something almost as good, if not as good as.'

'What?' said Fergus bluntly.

'It'll be a surprise,' said Louisa. So it would, starting with her and Robert. They were going to have to come up with something pretty *insolite*, that was certain. Fergus wouldn't forget. It was a jolly good thing that Regent Street was Louisa's front-yard.

53

'Oh, you're early!'

'Am I?'

'I mean, it isn't even dinner-time yet – look, I'm still cooking, it isn't even – '

'Well, I didn't say I'd be working late *every* night, did I?'

'Didn't you?'

'Where's the gin?'

'I think we might be out of tonic.'

'Rats. I'll go and get some.'

'I should have remembered – I just – '

'Never mind.' Simon went out, and returned twenty minutes later with a large carrier bag, which he put down on the kitchen table. Flora looked askance. He began unpacking. 'I thought we might as well have a party while I was about it,' he said. 'Just the five of us.'

'Oh how lovely.'

'Ask me why.'

'Why?'

'I've got Michael *and* Nathaniel.'

'Oh, *congratulations*. How wonderful.'

'Yes, it is that. And they're both dead keen. Nathaniel's dying to be a sweetie and Michael yearns to be a cad.'

'Marvellous.'

The constituents of the party were all now unpacked: the tonic for the gin-and, lemonade for the children, potato crisps, salted nuts and stuffed olives; *de luxe* chocolate ice-cream. 'This is for afters,' Simon said. 'Shall I shove it in the freezer?' He went and called the children and they all drank a toast to the Lloyd's names, Nathaniel's agent, Michael's agent, and Lizzie Ainsworth.

'And David,' said Flora. 'We mustn't forget David. He's the most important of the lot. The writer is the *sine qua non*.'

'A lot of use the writer would be,' said Simon, 'without the subject-matter, or the producer, or the actors, or etcetera.'

'He could just write novels,' said Janey. 'About love, or something. Then he wouldn't need all the rest.'

'Yes,' said Nell, 'that's right, he could, easily.'

'What's novels?' said Thomas.

'You know,' said Nell. 'Like *Winnie-the-Pooh*; that's a novel.'

'Oh,' said Thomas. 'I thought that was just a book.'

'He'd still need a publisher,' said Simon. '*If* he could find one. And then he wouldn't actually make any money. Not likely. So he's far better off as he is. Which he knows.'

'I might write a novel, one of these days,' said Thomas. 'Or a book.'

They all laughed, but Flora stopped when she saw his face. 'Yes, darling,' she said; 'I really think you might.'

Thomas drank some lemonade. 'Anyone could,' he said. 'There's no law against it.'

They all laughed again, but this time Thomas, uncertain about the cause but gratified by the result, joined in.

'I'm probably going to be an actress,' said Nell; and they all saw that indeed, she probably was, one way or another.

'It's a hard life,' Simon warned her.

'And what about our Janey,' said Flora. 'Any ambitions, darling?'

'Oh, I'm going to travel around the whole world,' said Janey. 'All of it. I want to see what it's *really* like.' And the younger children said that of course, they should do that too; that went without saying. And Flora and Simon each silently hoped that they really would, all of them, do just that; as long as they came back safely. You couldn't possibly bear to think of them going off, so far, and never coming back. Transience was all very well, but there were limits.

54

'Aren't you going to give me a guided tour?'

'If you like. Shall we start at the top?'

She started up the stairs and he followed her. Half-landing, more stairs, landing. Finest Wilton and gloss white, all spanking clean. More stairs, another half-landing, then the final ascent. Two empty rooms, and a tiny bathroom. 'These can be spare bedrooms,' she said. 'Or one can be a study. If I decide to take up studying.'

'You could. Seems a pity not to in the circs.'

'Well yes, I could. It could come to that.'

It could. Indeed it could.

'Let's go down then.' They descended to the first floor. 'Da-da,' she sang, flinging open a door. All the doors here were real doors, with panels and brass handles. The master bedroom: the larger room, overlooking the street; an en suite bathroom. The back room was a dressing room. He looked through the window on to the tiny garden, and saw Solomon sitting on the handkerchief-sized lawn amongst the fallen leaves. 'Ah, Solomon,' he said.

'Yes, Solomon's in clover. He's never been outside before. Not since he left his mother, at any rate.'

Simon looked down at the cat, who so well deserved the change in his fortunes. 'Good,' he said; 'good.' As they descended once more to the ground floor he suddenly realised that the sight of the bedroom, the bed itself, had left him quite unmoved.

She turned into the sitting room, which ran the length of the house, with french windows at the rear. There were a few pieces of furniture in it. 'I've acquired the fundamentals, as you see,' she said. 'I'll pick up the rest bit by bit.'

'Have some fun with it.'

'I mean to. See those alcoves?' He did, one each side of the fireplace. 'I'll have to think of something to put in them.'

'Books?'

She pulled a face. 'I was thinking more along the lines of statues.'

'Ah.'

'I'll see. And now come and see the kitchen.'

It was long and low-ceilinged, large enough to accommodate a dining table and chairs at one end – where more french windows led to the garden – and had all the latest equipment. 'Was all this stuff here?' he asked. There was, for example, a large and very splendid gas cooker.

She put a hand on it and nodded. 'This is French,' she said.

'Someone must have been very serious about cooking,' he said.

'Rather wasted on me,' she said sadly.

'You'll just have to get serious yourself,' he said. 'It's the only solution.'

'I could go to some classes, couldn't I?' she said brightly. Brightly, innocently; seriously. It wrenched his heart.

'Yes,' he said, 'you could. Good idea. The kitchen can be your study.'

'Yes,' she said eagerly, 'you know I think I really might.' And she looked almost delighted.

'That's settled, then,' he said; and now he suddenly, after

all, wanted her; he took her in his arms. At this moment the knowledge that he loved her possessed him so entirely that silence was painful; he held her very close until the pain ebbed away. Its ebbing was followed by a sadness, almost a sense of desolation. 'So you've managed everything,' he said.

'Yes; all sorted.'

'BT, Electricity, Gas?' he said.

'And the Water,' she said; 'all on stream, all on time.'

'Jolly good. These privatised monopolies done got *rhythm.*'

She laughed. She looked up at him. 'Well, do you like my house?' she said.

'It's perfect.'

'Yes, it *is,* isn't it?'

'I didn't know what to bring you. For a housewarming present.'

'Oh, but you've brought me yourself.'

He was left for the moment speechless; but then, 'As it were,' he said.

'As it were,' she repeated.

'Damn it all,' he said, and he began to kiss her. Later on, he saw the orchid that Rupert had sent; several frail white blooms on a long curving stem, growing in a clay pot. He hadn't realised that Rupert might actually care. Still, he, Simon, had her.

55

The vicar ascended the stairway into the pulpit; he crossed himself, In the name of the Father and of the Son and of the Holy Spirit, Amen, and then he looked around at his congregation, his church, his – our – his Father's – world; all the misery and the marvel and the mystery of it; '*Algebra*,' he said.

The silence was absolute. He looked down at them, concern and compassion on his face. 'Algebra,' he repeated. Then he raised his hands from the edge of the pulpit and pushing back the sleeves of his surplice slightly raised them into the air, as if writing on a blackboard.

'Three plus two,' he said, 'equals five. Three-plus-two-equals-five. That's arithmetic.' Pause. 'You know where you are, don't you, with arithmetic? Three plus two always equals five.' He was holding up five fingers. 'Good, straight-forward stuff. Pretty boring, of course. Not much to get your teeth into. No. Three plus two always and forever equals five. It's relentless, is arithmetic. No room for argument. It leaves you speechless.'

He paused, and looked down at them again, full of concern and compassion. They'd all suffered from arithmetic, and would again. Then he looked up, and over their heads, towards the organ loft, and beyond it, into the world, the universe.

'Whereas,' he said, 'algebra. *Algebra*. Ah, *now*: consider this.' And he waited for a second, to give the slower-witted time to gird up their loins, and consider. 'Two,' he began – and paused for another compassionate, rhetorical second, 'plus x – two plus x – equals five! Yes! Two plus x equals five: that is algebra. There it is. Two plus x equals five. And we will know, won't we, in this very simple, very elementary exercise that x here must equal three – we'll know this almost without having to think, won't we? If two plus x equals five then x, *in this instance*, equals three. So far so good.' He could only trust that it was.

'But of course, what most of us may remember about algebra is that it isn't usually so simple. No. We very soon get to the stage of dealing with more complicated propositions: simultaneous equations, and worse teasers still, where we have many many unknowns to find values for: x's and y's and even z's, squared and cubed and multiplied and divided until we hardly know where to turn, and it may not be boring but God knows we might even wish it were, because the fact is, it's *difficult*. We have to use our brains as hard as we can, haven't we? And even then we might not get the correct answer. Boring, no; difficult, yes; even impossible, at least for us, today, if not for someone else, today, or for us, next week, or next year.

'Because there is a way, isn't there? There is a method for doing these complicated sums in algebra: you only have to know the method, and apply it correctly, and you will find the answer in the end. The unknowns, the x's and y's and z's, will all be revealed for the quantities they actually are. You'll have *the answer*. It may take a long time. It may even take courage; it will almost certainly take patience; what it will very certainly take is faith – yes, *faith*.

'You knew I'd get around to that, didn't you? Some of you have been saying to yourselves, come along Vicar, you can't fool us. You can pretend to be talking about mathematics as much as you like but we know where you're going! So, very well: I'm here: faith.

'Because you're never going to start doing that piece of algebra, are you, without the faith that it *can* be done: that there *is* an answer; that it's not just a nonsense, that there is a method, and that if you follow the method correctly, you'll get the thing out in the end. Even when it's become so difficult that you feel you never will – you'll still keep trying. You might put it aside for a while, or sleep on it, or go and make a cup of tea and do something else for a while to clear your head; you might even go to someone else for a bit of advice, just to make sure you've got the method right; but you'll go back to it, and you'll go on trying to solve it, because you've got faith. You know where you're going *and why*.

'Well, I suppose some of you, not to say all of you, already know where I'm coming out now, don't you? You know I'm going to tell you that life, rather *living*, is like one of those problems in algebra. *It's not arithmetic, it's algebra.* It's full of unknowns. There are x's and y's and z's wherever you look, squared and cubed and multiplied and divided; and the people who tell you it's arithmetic are misleading you. It's algebra, and sometimes you have to be patient, and courageous. And sometimes *all* you have, the *only* thing you have, is your faith.

'And *those* are the times when you discover that faith, this simple thing, *is enough*. Yes. Is enough. Is everything. That the answer, the solution, can wait. That your ignorance is *assuaged* by your faith. Life, living, the world, is full of x's and y's and z's because God has made it so. These unknowns, these mysteries, are the places where He hides from us so that we may seek Him: for in the searching is the true finding.

'You see, it doesn't truly matter whether or not we find all the answers to all the mysteries. What truly matters is the act of searching — the faithful searching. Next Sunday is the first in Advent, when we begin once again our great search, like the shepherds and the wise men before us, for the babe born in a manger: for the Word made flesh: the great central mystery of our Christian faith. Let us now remember then that in our true and faithful searching is our finding. We may not know the whole solution of this mystery — perhaps we never can, this side of the grave. We are not doing arithmetic, which is boring, and which leaves us speechless. No; we are doing *algebra*, with all its x's and y's and z's: with all its unknowns. We live with the unknown, and even with the unknowable. But *by faith* we shall surely attain such knowledge as we can truly comprehend, by God's grace. In the name of the Father and of the Son and of the Holy Spirit, Amen.' And, having crossed himself once more, he turned and descended from the pulpit.

56

Simon was looking at six-by-eight glossies, with CVs attached, of actresses.

Simon was going to stick his neck out: he wanted some beauties. He was a bit tired of quirky, clever-looking actresses. If only they'd been all as clever as they were said to look, that might have been something. We British distrust beauty, he thought; we're suspicious even of prettiness. These girls would be nowhere in France or Italy. Just because some of our greatest actresses are plain doesn't mean that all must be. Or that plain actresses will always be great; or even good. He was going to find some beauties who could act if it killed him. This thing was meant to be *noir*, wasn't it? So he needed beauties. Who could act. He was going to put out a red alert first thing in the morning. Meanwhile it was Sunday and he was looking at six-by-eights of quirky clever-looking females who would never do. Not for him; not this time. 'Have a butcher's at these,' he said to Flora. She put down her needlework and held out a hand.

'Hmmm,' she said; 'hmmm, hmmm. I like this one best.'

Simon took the photograph and looked at it again. 'Imagine that face under a hat,' he said.

'Is that the test?' she asked. 'Will she be wearing a hat?'

'Maybe not,' said Simon. 'But I want hat faces.'

'Yes, I see,' said Flora. 'Hat faces.' They thought of all those hat faces of the cinematographic past. 'Maybe they don't make them any more,' she said. 'Since women stopped wearing hats. Since everyone stopped wearing hats, except for very special occasions.'

'There must be a few out there somewhere,' said Simon. 'And I'm going to find them.' And he was. 'Let's go out,' he said. The children had all gone out for the afternoon before them. They went to Kenwood House, and almost forgot when it was time to fetch Thomas. They had to go like the clappers. He grinned at her. 'That was fun, wasn't it?' he said, and she smiled guiltily back at him.

Thomas was waiting in front of the Kensington Odeon, where he'd been taken by the parents of a school friend along with said friend, holding the hand of the female parent, who was looking harried, on the verge of irritation. Thomas himself was looking just a little anxious.

'Do *please* forgive us,' said Flora. Simon was waiting around the corner with the car. 'We're *abject*.' That did the trick. Point to Mrs Beaufort. *Abject*. Thomas's friend's parents took their child home to a square in *echt* Kensington thinking that the Beauforts must be okay, really, even if they did live in Hammersmith. And then, it showed a certain self-assurance (just about as much as one ought to have, actually) to be late, just a little late, for a rendezvous of this kind. Furthermore, there was absolutely nothing wrong with Thomas himself. Thomas was a perfect little dear.

57

On the bedside table there was a shiny new copy of *Larousse gastronomique*. 'What on earth is that door-stopper doing there?' asked Simon, wide-eyed.

'Well, it's just my bed-time reading; you know.'

'You're joking, of course.'

'No, I'm entirely serious. It's fascinating. You know I told you I was going to learn to cook.'

'I thought you said you were going to go to some classes.'

'Yes, I am, too, but I thought first I'd better just do some limbering-up.'

He couldn't stop laughing, not for ages. She even began to look a little hurt; he had to make a real effort to stop.

'I don't think you're very kind,' she said.

He began laughing again. I love you, oh how I love you. 'Come here,' he said. But God, oh God, God help him: no: it wasn't enough. *It wasn't enough*; it wasn't the same. What kind of terrible paradox was this? That the act was less convincing, less powerful, less real, less true, than the words? How could this be? He held her in his arms, silent, astonished, appalled. My love, my love. 'Have you actually tried to cook anything yet?' he said.

'No; but I will.'

He could have laughed at that, too, five minutes ago, but nothing was funny any more. He felt at the moment that nothing could ever be funny again: that the sadness – almost horror – that he felt now would swamp his spirit forever. 'You're a funny girl,' he said.

She looked up at him. 'No, I'm not,' she said. 'Really, I'm not. I'm the least funny girl you ever met.' That look in her eyes again: as candid, as guileless as those of an animal, or a very young child. He was speechless, truly speechless. He held her in his arms. This was just no good. This was just no *effing* good. They had reached another stage – without warning, without any prior knowledge that such a state of affairs could even be – another stage: the final stage. He suddenly knew this. There was nothing more beyond this: not for them. Not as things were. He'd reached the end of the ever-finer line, and arrived at a blank wall. There it was, right in front of his nose. So perhaps they could just go on existing in this stage, being together, here, up against this blank wall. Was that possible? It was going to have to be. 'Shall we go out?' he said. 'Shall we go and have a drink in that brasserie?' There was nothing else, not another damned thing, that he could offer her.

58

Flora was looking happy – he suddenly saw this – for the first time for – how long? months? years? This was, at any rate, the first time he'd noticed it: that she was looking truly happy; she was smiling, laughing, joking with Thomas and Nell while she cooked the dinner. And she looked pretty. She was his own lovely Flora, she was what he'd seen her to be, known her to be, from the earliest moment, at that idiotic ball, years ago.

When all the children were in bed he sat beside her on the sofa and put his arms around her. She went on stitching as best she could. 'I'm trying to finish this one tonight,' she said; 'I'm so close.' She had just a little more sky to do.

'Well done,' he said, 'well done. Is that the lot?'

She stared at him, appalled. 'Oh no! there are still three more to go! I'll be just halfway.'

He laughed. 'You don't want to finish,' he said. 'You'll miss it.'

'Yes,' she agreed. 'I'll have to begin something else. I don't want to think about that now.' No: it wouldn't do to think about that now.

'How's your friend the Mother of God these days?'

She pulled a face. 'The confinement is due in just over a fortnight,' she said. 'As you will have noted.'

'Yes, I had.'

'So you must know as well as I how she is.'

'You never seem to mention the lady these days.'

'I'm in another stage.'

'I suppose you would be, at that. So, how's it going, round at St Thing's?'

'It's okay.'

'Truly?'

'It's nice.'

'As you said before.'

'Well, it is still.'

'I suppose that's something: still nice, after all these weeks.'

'Yes, I should have thought so.'

'What about that vicar?'

'Freddy.'

'*Freddy?*'

'Yes, Freddy.'

'I love it.'

'And his wife's called Phoebe. He calls her Phoebes, when they're alone together.'

'How do you know that?'

'I took some jumble round the other day, to the vicarage. They're having a jumble sale next Saturday. And he opened the door to me and called her. "I say, Phoebes," he said, "Flora's here with some jumble." So there.'

Simon was laughing. 'What a set-up,' he said, and laughed some more.

Flora was laughing too. 'I'm inclined these days to think that disestablishment would be a real pity,' she said.

'The joke would rather lose its edge,' Simon agreed.

'And not only that, either,' said Flora.

'Ah,' said Simon. 'Well, I wouldn't know about the rest.'

'Perhaps you don't know what you know.'

'Or even what I don't know.'

'There you go.'

'I hope you didn't give them anything of mine,' said Simon, remembering the jumble.

'Of course not,' said Flora. 'All the same, if you could find time before the end of the week to sort out anything you don't really need any more, or never wear – '

'I need it all. I wear it all.'

'Alright,' said Flora. 'Okay.'

'It's my jumble,' said Simon, 'and I'm going to keep it. So, you've reached the jumble-donating stage. There's Anglican for you. Can't get in much deeper than that.'

'You can,' said Flora, 'and I have: I'm going to help out at the sale itself. Nell's going to come with me; Janey's still thinking about it.'

'Well, I suppose I'd better plan to do something manly with Thomas, then,' said Simon, 'while you girls are jumbling.'

'That's the idea. Get him macho-ed up ready for Fergus.'

'*What?*'

'The school holidays start next week so Fergus is going to be coming here every day; we're minding him for Louisa. And for Robert, come to that.'

'I must say that seems frightfully good of you, Flora.'

'I suppose I simply am frightfully good. What an affliction.'

'We'll have to try and find a cure.'

'Going to church might do it.'

'Yes. I'll keep a watch. You actually mean to go on with it then, do you?' He wasn't laughing any more; he wasn't even smiling.

'It *is* a good way of recycling old clothes.'

'Oh well in that case.'

'That's my feeling.'

Simon was in truth more reassured than not by the news about the jumble: Flora could hardly be contemplating an eventual withdrawal, with the objective of re-grouping in the Church of Rome, if she was not only contributing to, but actually helping with the sale of, the Anglican jumble. 'You're not making a cake as well, are you?' he asked her.

'They did mention the possibility, in a general sort of way,' she said; 'but I explained to Phoebe that I didn't really have the time.'

'Ah,' said Simon, struggling to keep a straight face; 'I hope she excused you willingly.'

'Oh yes,' said Flora hastily. 'She understood perfectly. She's a working mum too, you see.'

'Oh really? You mean, as well as being Mrs Vicar?'

'Oh yes. As she said, they need the loot.'

'So what does she do?' What did clergymen's wives do – secretarial work? nursing?

'She's a theologian,' said Flora. 'She's a don at King's College London.'

'Oh I see,' said Simon. 'Of course.'

'Look!' said Flora. 'It's finished!' And she held up the piece of tapestry, one day to be a dining chair seat-cover: a silent creamy mollusc shell before a stormy froth-fringed sea.

59

'How's your autonomy?'

'It seems alright to me.'

'As long as you've been remembering to look.'

'I haven't had time actually to look, but I'm sure if anything were amiss I'd know soon enough.'

'I'll leave it with you then.'

'By definition.'

'I'm going to be a bit tied up over the next few weeks or so. I suppose you are too.'

'I hadn't particularly looked at the next few weeks or so.'

'Christmas, you see.'

'Oh that.'

'Major festival.'

'Even the stockmarket pulls down the shutters.'

'Had you any plans?'

'Mother.'

'Oh, right.'

She sat up and lit a cigarette. 'Then there's New Year,' she said.

'Always that.'

'I'll be away for a fortnight around then,' she went on; 'skiing.'

'Another of Rupert's shows, I suppose?'

'Rupert *et al*. Chalet party.'

'I can just picture it.' She shrugged, as it were dis-

missively; 'It's nice up in the mountains,' she said. 'I love
snow.'

'That's good.'

'Yes. Will you miss me?'

'No. I'll be too busy. Will *you* miss *me*?'

'No. I'll be too busy too.'

'That's settled then. Shall we have another meal together,
at the end of the week, say – for – '

'Yes, why not.'

'We might go to that place of ours on Thursday night;
can you manage that?'

'Yes, I can manage that.'

Then they would come back here again, electrified by the
particular charge that was built up only in these circumstances, of being in a public place together. There was so
little scope for improvisation, so very little. Here they were,
just the two of them, dancing their mystical dance together
unwitnessed, unannounced. It had a certain purity, of course.
It had an awful purity. It remained to be seen whether they
were, whether the dance itself was, great enough for the
circumstances; grand enough to sustain the glare of that awful
purity.

60

Lydia and Louisa were in Soho again eating salt-beef sandwiches. 'Although I shouldn't,' said Louisa. 'I'm meant to be
on a diet.'

'A diet? *Now?*'

'Saves going on one after. I always try to lose half a stone
just before Christmas.'

'I always try to lose half a stone, full stop.'

'Idiot. Love the jacket, is it new?'

'Yes – Flora's jumble sale. Sort of early fifties, don't you
think? Look at this lining.'

'Yes, I say, it's your actual satin. Scrummy. Is there a label?'

'Deréta.'

'You *were* lucky.'

'Was I not? Listen, Louisa, I have to tell you something.'

'Tell away.'

'You probably won't thank me.'

'Try me.'

'I have to tell someone, you see.'

'I'm right here.'

'Remember how I saw Simon that time in Westbourne
Grove.'

'In the Volvo.'

'Yeah. Well – the other night, I'm walking along one of
those back streets off Queensway, because I've been visiting
that photographer of mine whom I mentioned before.'

'Yes, that one.'

'And so I'm going to go down and hop on a number 36 which isn't an awful lot of use but it's better than nothing, which is the alternative.'

'Yes, yes. You really need a car.'

'I know, but I can't face the bother just yet. Anyway, I'm walking along – '

'Walking along, yes.'

'In the night.'

'Have to be careful.'

'Are you kidding? And I just sort of vaguely notice this couple, several yards ahead of me, also walking along; and there's just something about them – they're not holding hands, or anything, but you can just tell – you know what I mean. They're *together*. You could take a photograph, of this back view, and call it 'lovers'; but you wouldn't even have to label it for anyone to simply *know*, straightaway. Rather beautiful, really.'

'Yes. Lovely. But?' Louisa was all serious attention. The story had after all been flagged.

'And so I was just vaguely thinking – you know how one does – well I suppose *you* don't, as you've got Robert – '

'Who's a lover in a hundred – '

'And witty with it: so I was vaguely thinking – ah, *nice work if you can get it* – the way a woman like me would – when they stopped walking along, and turned in at that brasserie there – which come to think of it you probably wouldn't know of. There's this newish brasserie just along there, rather nice. So in they went; but of course they were dithering in the doorway long enough for me to see that the chap was someone I actually knew. Simon, in fact. Simon Beaufort.'

'And the chapess was not, I take it, Flora.'

'Not even slightly.'

'I see.'

The two women sat there, feeling horrible. 'Actually,' said Lydia, 'I feel worse now I've told someone, not better.'

Louisa said nothing for a moment. 'Still,' she said, 'one would have to tell someone. I do see that.'

'And it really did have to be you,' said Lydia. 'I mean – '

'Yes, I see that too,' said Louisa. 'Did this happen after the jumble sale, or before?'

'Oh, after, thank God,' said Lydia. 'Thursday night, actually. I mean, if it had been before – '

'You might not be wearing that jacket.'

'Possibly not.'

'As it is – '

'There's absolutely nothing one can do,' said Lydia. 'Apart from sharing the burden of the knowledge, so to speak. I mean, there's nothing practical one can do, nothing. I've thought and thought. It's simply out of the question.'

Louisa thought too. 'Yes,' she said. 'That's right. It is.'

'Of course,' said Lydia slowly, 'you have only my word for it. They might not be lovers. There might be a perfectly innocent explanation.'

Louisa's face brightened for a moment but then became serious again. 'Let's just say so, for the moment,' she said. 'Let's suppose it was entirely innocent – shall we?'

'I suppose we *could*,' said Lydia. 'I suppose I *could* say that I imagined their being lovers: a projection from the rich fantasy life of a celibate woman-of-a-certain-age, etcetera. That could certainly be a possibility. Shall we say that?'

'She's just some actress he's sussing out for this new series he's directing,' said Louisa. 'He took her in there to see how she'd look in a restaurant. Flora told me he's being very particular about the women for this thing; he wants beauties.

Hat faces, he said. So she told me. Did this woman have a hat face?'

'I'm not sure . . . possibly, I suppose. Possibly.' She hadn't; not in Lydia's estimation. But there was no need to say so categorically. It was a minor point. The revised interpretation held water just sufficiently without it.

'So she's an actress,' said Louisa, 'and you have a rich fantasy life, okay? Right so far?'

'Right,' said Lydia. 'And Simon's getting on with the job.'

'Right,' said Louisa. 'So come back to the shop with me and help me choose something absolutely *wonderful* to give Flora, for looking after Fergus.' Which they did.

61

Nell was definitely coming; Janey supposed she would; Thomas, getting wind of their plans, was ready to promise anything, even unto having a sleep in the afternoon beforehand, in order to come too. 'Oh, I don't know,' said Simon. 'It's hardly my sort of thing.' But at the last moment he shrugged on his coat and started switching off the unstrategic lights. 'I might as well,' he said. 'As long as you're all going.' And so they all went to the midnight mass on Christmas Eve.

'We've never done this before,' said Flora happily, a daughter on either arm – Nell all pleased excitement, Janey all mild curiosity.

'That's because I wasn't old enough last year,' said Thomas. 'But now I am.'

'That must be it,' Flora agreed.

Of course, once they were actually in the candlelit church, and the nine-lessons-and-carols part of the programme had begun, there was no doubting the propriety of the outing; not even Janey, not even Simon, could doubt it now. Nell was entranced; Thomas was awestruck; Janey's curiosity, if it was not thoroughly aroused, ceased in any case to be merely mild. Simon, looking around at the singing congregation, acknowledged for a moment the presence of something more than harmless delusion – whether dangerous delusion, or harmless truth, or dangerous truth, he would not dare determine.

During the celebration of the Eucharist itself he began to think that if this were a representation of a truth, then this truth itself might indeed be dangerous in one sense or another: for see how it was represented! It won't do, he thought. It must not do. He was quite sure about this. He glanced at Janey. She watched the proceedings, impassive: Janey won't fall for it, he thought. And he needn't worry about the younger children yet.

But as he was thinking these thoughts a bell once more rang and he saw that people were getting up and filing towards the sanctuary to receive the sacrament. He glanced along at Flora, who sat immobile, leaning slightly forward, merely watching. That's something, he thought. But he was too hasty, for in the next second Flora, frowning slightly, spoke briefly to Thomas and then rose from her seat and went out into the aisle and took her place in the queue. Good God. She was going to commune: here, now, in front of them all. He glanced, appalled, at the children – Thomas, next to Flora's vacant place, Nell beside him and then Janey.

As he did so, Thomas slithered off his seat and, having thwarted Nell's attempt to detain him, went and stood behind his mother, whose sleeve he tugged at to announce his presence. There was a whispered argument which finished with Thomas's remaining where he was; whereupon Nell followed him.

Janey now looked at her father, raised her eyebrows, shrugged, and followed her sister; and Simon could only sit there and watch while his wife and children slowly filed towards the front of the church. Well, he thought, the children can't actually receive, they haven't after all been confirmed. Of course they'd been baptised, solely to please their grandparents: 'It's the least one can do,' as his mother had said: and in this matter Simon was all, as he had told her, for doing the least one could. But what on earth had possessed them to follow their mother like this? Why hadn't they simply waited here with him? The thought of a hen and her chicks came to mind.

Flora now took her place in the row of communicants, Thomas before her and Nell and Janey either side. As far as Simon could make out, the celebrant had managed to comprehend their situation, and simply made the sign of the cross with the wafer over each child before giving it to Flora, but even this looked like a brush with danger to Simon. Suddenly he understood that for all its barminess and ineptitude, this church – even this – existed for the sake of a delusion, or a truth – whichever it might be – which was, in fact, dangerous: dangerous to the world as it was, as it so precariously was. It had changed the world-as-it-was before and it might, it just conceivably *could*, do so again; and the point is, thought Simon, things are dodgy enough as they are, without a revolution. The last thing we can deal with now is a revolution.

But then, he thought, after all, it's hardly likely. Almost no one's paying attention. How many people ever enter a church, even tonight – how many more stay away? There will be no revolution. Cheer up! It's Christmas, after all! And he watched his family coming back up the aisle: Thomas, looking delighted with himself, Nell, looking pious, Janey, looking inscrutable, and Flora, looking – how? Well, Flora looked like Flora. Which in this transitory world was more, very much more, than one could ever have dared to ask.

62

On New Year's Day the Beauforts were At Home. There was a huge ham, salads, bread, biscuits, cheese, trifle (made by Janey, with some assistance from Nell), Bucks Fizz and blanc de blancs; and the major part of the Christmas cake.

There were adults getting rather sloshed – 'Hair of the dog, old thing' – small children running and yelling, women nattering together, music playing *much too loud* in Janey's room – where she and her friends Amaryllis and Katie were holed up conspiratorially – and Alex Maclise and like-minded cronies getting stoned, or so they hoped. Most of the actors were there, and their partners where applicable, and David and Sarah, and the designer. So was Lizzie, and Alfred, and their daughter Henrietta, one of the chief runners and yellers; and also Louisa and Robert, *sans* the notorious Fergus, he having gone to stay with his grandparents as projected. So Louisa had plenty of time to attend to the Beauforts.

'How's everything going, Simon?'

'Can't complain, Louisa; can't complain.'

'How's your new thing shaping up?'

'Looking pretty good so far, touch wood.'

'Are all these strange lovelies your female players?'

'Some of them, some of them. See if you can pick them out. You want three.'

Louisa picked. Could one of these women actually be the female sighted by Lydia in the vicinity of Queensway that night? Impossible to tell. Did Simon have the indefinable air of the adulterer? Equally. How unfortunate that Lydia herself was absent.

'Flora's looking awfully well,' she said.

'Yes, isn't she,' Simon agreed.

'I was afraid,' Louisa went on, 'I might find her in shreds. After two weeks of Fergus. Give or take.'

'Oh, Flora's made of strong stuff,' said Simon. 'Flora can cope. Flora is the cat's whiskers.' Was there just a hint of complacency in his tone? Not that that in itself was indicative, one way or the other.

'Yes,' Louisa said, 'I believe you're right.'

'Damn sure I am,' said Simon with finality. Louisa cast around for another leading question, studying Simon's half-averted face the while for signs of duplicity or deceit, but had managed nothing better than to ask him whether it was in fact Auntie, or the other lot, who had had the privilege of buying in the new series, when there was a distraction.

Simon had been keeping half an eye on Thomas, who had fallen into conversation with some of the actors; he could now clearly be heard offering to show them his rendition of the hornpipe and almost immediately therafter be seen donning his ballet shoes – which he had just happened to have with him – and providing the proferred entertainment.

This was bad enough, at least in his parents' eyes, but before they could gracefully put an end to the performance one of the actors stood up and asked Thomas very nicely to show him how it was done. 'Oh, me too!' cried another; and within a few seconds Thomas had several large pupils all begging for instruction.

'Oh no,' Thomas told them. 'You've got to do your *pliés* first.'

'Oh, please, Thomas,' they cried, 'do let us off our *pliés*. We want to dance!'

Thomas looked very shocked, and altogether determined. 'No,' he said severely. 'You're not allowed to do *anything* before you do your *pliés*. It's a *rule*.'

'Oh dear. Then I suppose we'll have to do our *pliés*. Shall we?' They all agreed that they should do their *pliés*. Some were rather drunk and some were rather stoned but they all began, holding on to each other for support, to do their *pliés*, while Thomas on the sidelines criticised their hand positions.

'Not like that,' he said. 'Like this. See my hand?' Great play was made of the hand positions. 'And your feet are wrong, too,' said Thomas to another. They were no good at all. 'Try to keep in time,' he told them, singing the tune used for *pliés* at his class. There was much shrieking and groaning but he told them at last that they could stop.

'Now for the hornpipe,' they cried. 'Show us, Thomas!'

'Perhaps you should do some *tendus* as well,' said Thomas uncertainly.

'No, no *tendus*, not today,' they begged, 'we haven't time. Show us the hornpipe.'

So he relented, and began. 'Watch me carefully,' he told them.

It was pretty simple stuff, but my God how they got it wrong! Within seconds they were all outdoing each other in hopeless incompetence and lunatic improvisation, while Thomas laboured to correct them, singing the tune to them the while; and the more they got it wrong, the funnier – funnier! it wasn't even slightly funny to begin with, if you asked Thomas – they found it, as did those who were watching them, until they all collapsed back on to the sofa where they'd begun, or the floor around it, in a heaving helpless heap. Laugh! They nearly *died*.

Simon marched over to them and picked up his bewildered son and swung him around in a half circle. He could only just manage it – Thomas's infantile phase was now pretty well concluded. 'Nice work, old chap,' he said. 'Good try. Now you know what it's like working with actors. Dreadful, aren't they? Frightful people. Won't listen. Can't learn. *Hopeless*.'

'Oh, not fair!' the actors cried. 'We did try. We were doing our *very* best.'

Thomas, still in his father's arms, looked down at them pensively. 'Well,' he said; 'don't give up the day jobs.' Laugh? They nearly died, again. *Much* more nearly.

63

'The Beauforts seemed in good form,' said Louisa to Robert, later on, *chez eux*.

'Hmmm,' said Robert; 'yes.'

'Flora looked quite lovely.'

'Hmmm.'

'Didn't you think?'

Robert looked up. He was still holding the magnifying glass through which he had been looking at some ancient Greek coins which had been collected by his grandfather. 'What?' he said.

'Oh dear,' said Louisa. 'I knew you weren't really listening.'

'I was, *really*,' said Robert.

'What was I talking about, then?'

'Ah, now that was just what wasn't quite clear to me.'

'Although you were *really* listening.'

'I was waiting for you to get to the point, you see. I was sure there'd be one, sooner or later.'

'How would you have known when I reached it, if you were only *really* listening.'

'Well, your voice would have changed. Naturally.'

'I give up.'

'No, don't do that. Just tell me *exactly* what you want to say.'

'Well then. Lydia told me this story.' Louisa retailed it,

laying out both the alternative interpretations, as adumbrated in the salt-beef bar.

Robert listened, his gaze fixed on the coins. 'Hmmm,' he said.

'Hmmm? Is that all you can say, hmmm?'

'Seems entirely adequate to me.'

'You think she was just an actress, then.'

'*Could* be, I suppose. Could be. But no, I think on balance that the other interpretation is the likelier.'

'You do?'

'Yes, on balance.'

Louisa was astounded: she had expected Robert to choose the less sensational version, he being in her eyes the epitome of the rational not to say sceptical intelligence. Robert was employed by the Bank of England in work so esoteric that the layperson could have no hope of grasping what it entailed, even less what benefit it conferred and on whom; Robert had therefore, and for other cause too, the reputation of one who could not be distracted or deceived. 'You think, then,' she said wonderingly, 'that Simon Beaufort is actually having an affair.'

Robert picked up another coin and peered at it. 'Chaps like that are bound to have extra-marital love affairs,' he said. 'Or so the statistics indicate.'

'What *can* you mean?'

'One reads of these surveys, showing the incidence per thousand of population of adulterous liaisons. Startlingly high, as a matter of fact. Now, since chaps like me *don't*, chaps like Simon *must*.'

'When you put it like that,' said Louisa weakly. Robert said nothing, but went on peering at his coin. Then Louisa had a thought. 'How do you know,' she said, 'that chaps like you don't?'

'Too boring,' said Robert. 'Or too busy, or both.'

'But you're not boring.'

'I am busy, though.'

This was undeniable. The Bank of England was a hard mistress. 'I should be grateful for that,' said Louisa faintly.

Robert stopped peering at the coin and looked at her, still holding the magnifying glass. 'The rules about fidelity were made by chaps like me,' he said. 'We really meant them to be kept. We really thought that having such rules, and observing them, was more important than what is now called self-expression. Or self-realisation. Or whatever it is. Steady, dutiful, tidy, conscientious chaps we are. Completely lacking in charm and gaiety, of course. We leave all that sort of thing to our womenfolk, bless 'em. But you know all this.'

'Ye-e-es,' said Louisa. 'But meanwhile, supposing that gay and charming Simon is having it off with another woman, what about poor Flora?'

'What, indeed.'

'It makes me feel quite queasy.'

'There's a lot to be said for the rules.'

'Yes,' said Louisa sadly. 'Practically everything, really.'

64

'I wasn't sure you'd be back yet.'

'I got back a few days ago.'

'For some reason I thought you were due at the end of the week.'

'The beginning, as it happens.'

'I'm sorry.'

'It doesn't matter.'

It mattered like hell: or something did. She was slaloming away from him, out of his sight – one minute beside him, the next, with an awful *whoosh*, gone. Or so he felt.

'I thought you'd have a snow tan.'

'Didn't you know? That's not fashionable any more. We all cover up like mad with factor 25.'

'Oh, I see.' Do we all cover up together: do we all cover each other, laughing companionably, conspiratorially, all together, up on our mountain peaks? What the hell.

'So you had a good time?'

'Super.'

'That's good.'

'How about you?'

'I had a good time too.'

The family, and the fairy lights; the Christmas tree with the three children around it, their faces bathed in enchantment. Friends, and feasts, and parcels; shrieks of infant joy. The present for Flora: the very, very special present for

Flora. Happy Christmas, my dearest. 'Super,' she said. 'Would you like a drink? I've got some duty-free malt whisky here.'

'Wouldn't say no to that.'

They drank. It really was the business, wasn't it? She was like an ice queen whom he couldn't touch. It was worse than starting at the very beginning again. He looked at her. 'I don't know what to do,' he heard himself saying.

She looked back at him. 'In what sense?' she said.

He looked into his glass. Then he looked very seriously, steadily, at her. 'What do you think?' he said. 'What do you think we should do?'

She shrugged. 'What's all this *should*, all of a sudden?' she asked. 'When did we ever bother with *should*?'

'Fair question,' he said. So it was.

'Would you rather stop seeing me?'

'No.' Would he? No.

'Then it's quite clear, isn't it?'

'Clear enough,' he said. Not quite clear, but clear enough.

'Have another drink,' she said, pouring.

'Not too much, I'm driving.'

'Ah, yes.' He drank. She got up again and drew the curtains and then sat down once more, and waited for him to act. She could of course have taken the initiative, but she didn't so choose. Simon understood all this, waiting, as the minutes went by, for the time to arrive when he could naturally, authentically, act – and wondering, as the minutes went by, where, exactly, he was. The line had become so fine that he couldn't bloody see it any more; could only guess, moment by moment, where it might be. Assuming, of course, that it was actually there at all.

65

Flora had a system. As soon as her children were ten years old, they were allowed to earn extra pocket money by doing household chores over and above the tidying of their rooms on the accomplishment of which task payment of the basic dole itself depended. 'You don't get owt for nowt,' said Flora.

'It's not fair,' said Nell.

'What's not fair?'

'Just because she's thirteen,' said Nell, 'she's getting all that extra money for cleaning the baths and basins. It's not fair.'

'And I do some of the kitchen cleaning too,' said Janey. 'Not just the baths and basins.'

'You see?' said Nell. 'I know how to clean those things. I could do it easily.'

'Of course you couldn't,' said Janey. 'You're too young.'

'I'm afraid you couldn't, darling,' said Flora. 'Not properly.'

Nell looked almost tearful. 'It's not fair,' she said. It was a wonderful system, alright, where children begged for employment as domestics.

'And so could I,' said Thomas.

Nell turned on him. 'No you could not,' she said. 'You're *much* too young.'

'Much too young yourself,' said Thomas. 'Much – too – *young.*'

'Belt up both of you,' said Flora. 'It's no good having rules, Nell, if they're not kept, and this is a rule. Even ten is quite young. And it's only a few months away. May. Less than six months. Enjoy your childhood while you can.'

'I want to grow up,' said Nell.

Flora looked at her steadily. 'Show me your homework,' she said. Nell went to fetch it, and Flora had a look. Poor, precious little Nell.

'Why don't *I* ever get any homework?' asked Thomas. 'It's not fair.' His mother and sisters all laughed. 'Well it isn't,' he said. 'It isn't *fair*.'

'You might get some next year,' said Flora encouragingly.

'Fergus gets it,' said Thomas.

'There you are, then,' said Flora. 'He's only a few years older than you.'

'He's only three years older,' said Thomas. 'And he stays up late, too, and watches television after nine o'clock. And he goes swimming by himself, *in the sea*, and he shoots, too, in the country.'

'I wouldn't believe quite everything Fergus tells you,' said Flora.

'He does shoot, though,' said Thomas. 'He told me that particularly.'

'Well,' said Flora, 'I'm afraid that was fanciful. It's against the law, for a start, for someone of that age.'

'Fergus doesn't care about the law,' said Thomas.

'Yes, I noticed that,' said Flora. 'It's a jolly good thing that the law cares about Fergus.'

'Does the law care about me?' said Thomas.

'The law cares about all of us,' said Flora. 'In one way or another.'

They discussed the law, until it was Thomas's bed-time; and later, Nell's; and at last, Janey's; so passed another evening in the Beaufort household when Simon missed the children, and they, of course, him. Flora sighed, and began a new piece of tapestry; then she watched *Newsnight* (Paxo up) and went to bed. I'm not really worried, she told herself; I'm not really anxious. Nothing is wrong, *really*. That is – I've done all I can. I'm sure I've done all that I possibly can.

66

'The thing I never really noticed before,' said Simon to David, 'is that you start off by doing one thing, but pretty soon you find that you're actually doing something entirely different.'

'Yes, I think I know what you mean,' said David. 'More or less.'

'I mean,' said Simon, doggedly, 'that whatever your expectations are, whatever your suppositions are, they're bound to be inadequate – I mean, the reality you end up with is always different from anything you could have foreseen. And you sort of wake up one day and you look around you, at this situation you've got yourself into, and you say, *how the fuck* did I end up here?'

'And then you try to get the hell out,' said David.

'No,' said Simon; 'no, not necessarily. But even if you do – the point of the joke is, that even if you were to get out, you'd end up in the same basic situation – i.e., one you couldn't have foreseen – asking the same question all over again: what the fuck, etcetera.'

'Yes,' said David. 'I think I know what you mean.'

'Sure you do,' said Simon. 'You know what I mean.'

'My round,' said David. 'Same again?' Blimey, he thought, as he went over to the bar to get the drinks.

He came back with the two full glasses and some crisps. 'Get stuck in,' he said to Simon. 'Salt and vinegar. They didn't have any hedgehog flavour, I'm afraid. Don't know what this place is coming to.' Simon ignored the crisps and picked up one of the glasses and drank. David, after a second's hesitation, stealing a glance at Simon's face, picked up the other and did likewise. 'That was a good party of yours the other day,' he said. 'Sarah was going to send a note – hope she did. Note to Flora. Lovely Flora.' He raised his glass ever so slightly, stealing another quick glance at Simon the while.

'Yes,' said Simon, 'she is that. Got lucky there.' And with these words his face became quite intensely gloomy.

Double blimey, thought David. 'Kids looking pretty *pukkah* too,' he said. 'Got lucky there as well, what?'

'Yeah,' said Simon. 'I don't deserve it.'

David laughed. 'As if deserts had anything to do with it,' he said.

Now Simon laughed too. 'Can't think what's got into me,' he said. 'Must be all this churchgoing. I knew it was dangerous.'

'It's alright for women,' David said. 'They can handle it. But it's all a bit much for us men. We're not up to it. Not good enough for it, I suppose. It only confuses us. Better leave it to Flora and the kids.'

'I *suppose* it's alright for Flora,' said Simon doubtfully.

'Put it this way,' said David. 'She's so good already, it can't really make any difference, can it?'

'I suppose not,' said Simon, still doubtfully. 'I just – don't – know. It *could* be one of those situations where you don't know what's actually involved until it's too late. Quite *apart* from the fact that we *could* end up with a plastic Virgin Mary lit up from the inside and a full-colour photograph of the Pope in a frame and the whole bang shoot.'

'No,' said David, 'I shouldn't really think it'll come to that. Not Flora. No way. I wouldn't worry. Forget it.'

'Okay,' said Simon. But you couldn't be altogether confident that he would.

'How are those actors behaving themselves?' said David.

'Oh, they're brilliant,' said Simon. 'I have to say, they're brilliant.'

'Brilliant casting,' said David. 'That's what it is.'

'Yes,' said Simon. 'That must be it.'

'Cheer up, old cock,' said David.

'Sure thing,' said Simon. 'Have another?'

67

'Can't think what's got into Simon,' said David to Sarah. 'I wouldn't have put him down as the introspective sort, would you?'

'All artists are introspective, aren't they?'

'You'd call him an artist, then, would you?'

'Isn't a director an artist?'

'Er, I'm not sure.'

'Of course he is.'

'I'll bet Cecil B. de Mille wasn't introspective.'

'Bet he was.'

'Busby Berkeley?'

'Obviously. Don't be dense.'

'But *Simon*? Simon *Beaufort*?'

'Him too. Anyway, what was he introspecting about?'

'Oh, you know, life, that sort of thing.'

'Poor Simon.'

'Poor *what*?'

'You know, you get that feeling – it could all go so wrong.'

'What on earth are you talking about?'

'You know, Simon – there's this knife-edge feeling, with blokes like him; everything looks so cushy – well, cushy enough – but you get this feeling that, well, one false move – one moment of inattention, or one small miscalculation – and it could all go *so wrong*.'

'Well, surely it's the same for all of us. Chaos theory.'

'Yes, of course, but with Simon – with chaps like that – it's more precarious. More of a knife edge. Really – well – no room for error. None. No give in the system. Know what I mean?'

'I can't think why you should feel this particularly about Simon, for God's sake.'

'No, I don't either, particularly. I just do.'

'I suppose you're being intuitive, Sarah. You want to watch that.'

'Oh, I do.'

'Simon, eh. Well, just as long as he doesn't fall off his knife edge before he finishes my thing.'

'Oh, no. He'll finish that no matter what.'

'That's alright then.'

'I hope he'll be okay. I like Simon. He's a sweetie, really.'

'Is he?'

'I reckon so.'

'You're being intuitive again.'

'What else can a woman do?'

'She can be Prime Minister.'

'Better she should stick to being intuitive.'

'Amen!'

68

'This is a surprise.'

'Don't you like surprises?'

'Sometimes.'

'This time?'

'I'm not sure.'

'I'll make you sure. I'll make absolutely sure you're sure – ' He took her in his arms; he made quite sure that she would like this surprise.

'Are you sure now?' he said.

'Yes,' she said, 'I think so.'

'That's good,' he said. He lit a cigarette. She took it from him and smoked it for a while. Long shifting columns of light slithered across the ceiling and then vanished as cars passed in the street below. It was the hour of cars passing, on their urgent way to something important. Suddenly she turned from him and switched on the bedside lamp.

'I've got a photograph here of me on skis,' she said; 'do you want to see?'

He held the photograph and stared at it for a long time. *You can keep it, if you like. Oh – could I?* No, none of that. No pictures, no keepsakes, no presents; no traces. Nothing, nothing but the dance, and the dead indifferent wall. 'Very nice,' he said. It was, too. Whether by accident or design, it captured the entire *esprit* of the skiing classes (English division) at play. 'Which one is Rupert?' he said.

'Rupert took the picture.'

'Useful man.'

She laughed. 'He will soon be even usefuller,' she said. 'He's decided to come to cookery classes with me.'

'Oh?'

'Oh yes – I don't think I told you, did I – it all starts next week. Cookery on Tuesday nights, wine-appreciation on Thursdays. Thought we might as well whole-hog it; you get a reduction in the fees if you sign up for the two.'

'Thinking of opening a restaurant afterwards, are you?'

'Who knows?' she said. 'Tuesdays and Thursdays, eh,' he said, not laughing.

'Yes.'

'I see.'

'Just for six weeks. To start with, anyway. That's the elementary stage. After that, we'll see.'

'Where does all this take place?'

'A *comme il faut* little establishment quite nearby. A rather famous *comme il faut* little establishment, actually. Looks like a pretty cosy little earner to me. If Albie were to hear of it he'd probably try to buy a share in it.'

'Jolly good.'

'Yes, I can't wait.' She looked genuinely pleased and happy. She truly couldn't wait. She was going to wear an apron and hold a wooden spoon. And for the next six weeks at least if he wanted to see her on a Tuesday or a Thursday he could forget it. *Do you still love me?*

'Time I was going,' he said, getting up. She sat up and watched him dress, and then she reached for the pink silk kimono with the flying cranes and put it on, and got up herself. She twisted her hair up at the back and pinned it.

'I should be getting a move on myself,' she said. She went into the bathroom and turned on the bath taps and then came back into the bedroom. 'So cosy here, isn't it?' she said happily. All the rooms were so very much smaller than those in the mansion flat; all so close together. She sat down at the dressing table and began covering her face with cold cream.

'Are you going out somewhere?' he asked her.

She turned around. 'Mmmm,' she said. 'Meeting someone for dinner. Must hurry.' She started wiping off the cold cream and then turned around again. 'Could you be a sweetie and turn that bath off for me?' she said. 'I keep forgetting how much quicker it fills up than the old one.' The bath was smaller, too. The bathroom was full of heavily scented steam. When he came back into the bedroom she was standing in front of the wardrobe, looking at her dresses, choosing what to wear.

'Who's the lucky man?' he said.

'Who says it's a man?'

'Oh.'

'Although as a matter of fact, it is.'

'Ah.'

'Just a chap. Just another City type.'

'As long as he's worth all this effort.'

She had taken out an important-looking silk dress and was considering it carefully. 'I've got to keep my hand in,' she said. He was on the edge of rage: he could have torn the dress from her hand and flung it out of the window, thrown her across the room, shaken her until her teeth rattled, slapped her pale, almost plain face; instead he simply said, 'I'll leave you to it then. Enjoy yourself.' He even managed to put his arm briefly around her waist and kiss her cheek as he passed her on the way to the door.

She looked up and smiled. 'Thank you,' she said, her gaze as candid as a child's, or an animal's. 'Do you mind awfully seeing yourself out?'

'Of course not,' he assured her. 'Good night. Must dash.'
He ran down the stairs and strode along the passageway. At
the end of it, just by the front door, Solomon sat in a crouch.
As Simon approached, he rose to his feet and then standing
on his toes arched his back, and then subsided, his head
lifted, his gaze on Simon, as candid as a child's – staring,
finding no fault, no merit, only the world as it was, in all its
immense, impenetrable mystery.

69

'So what did you think?'

'Well, everything looked pretty good to me. Kids thriving; Flora in the pink; Simon — well, Simon was his usual quasi-seigneurial self, no more no less.'

'No signs of evasion or duplicity?'

'None that I could see.'

'Perhaps everything really is alright, then.'

'Possibly. But I should tell you that Robert thinks otherwise.'

'*What?*'

Louisa retailed her conversation with her husband. 'You should have been there,' she said. 'Then we would have known whether or not *she* was there too.'

'Yes,' said Lydia, 'it's a drag, isn't it: but I had to visit the pater.' The New Year visit was an annual chore, best accomplished without prevarication or alteration to the schedule. 'Anyway,' she went on, 'even if she had been there, that wouldn't necessarily have told us anything.'

'Her not being there might have done.'

'But not necessarily.'

'Actually we really don't know anything much, do we?'

'And we can't, unless we catch them *in flagrante.*'

'Which God forbid.'

'I'll tell you one thing I've remembered,' said Lydia, 'thinking it over.'

'What's that?'

'Her clothes. They really weren't at all what I'd call actress's clothes.'

'Oh. What kind were they?'

'Seriously expensive.'

'Nice or nasty?'

'Nice.'

'I *see*.'

'Doesn't look good, does it?'

'There's probably a perfectly innocent explanation, all the same,' said Louisa. 'There *must* be. *Pace* Robert and the old statistics.'

'Wish we knew it. I do hate a mystery.'

'Infuriating, isn't it?'

'And it could be something an awful lot worse.'

'Let's just hope not,' said Louisa.

'Absolutely,' said Lydia.

70

He'd have to be careful, damned careful, now that Tuesdays and Thursdays were out, not to fall into a pattern. He'd have to watch it. He was actually having to work pretty late anyway once or twice a week, depending. So one way or another, he was very likely going to be seeing even less of Gillian than heretofore – for the next six weeks, at least. But it couldn't really matter: it could never be allowed, or at any rate admitted, really to matter. And in fact, he assured himself, it doesn't matter. How could it?

So here he was, on a night when he might have come home from work via Bayswater, and missed Thomas, and even Nell, and even Janey, sitting down to dinner with all three, and, of course, Flora, who did it every single night. And it was where he belonged, no doubt about that; it was where he manifestly and unquestionably belonged. That, perhaps, was the whole problem.

After the children were all in bed Flora picked up a book and started reading it.

'What are you reading?'

'It's one of the novels Claire brought me.'

'Oh yes; Claire's review copies.'

'It must be nice, getting all the new novels.'

'I should think it would be a total pain in the neck; I don't know why she doesn't just flog the lot.'

'She flogs some of them, she only keeps the good ones.'

'What about that one you're reading, then? Good, is it?'

'We-e-ell – '

'There you are then.'

'I just wanted to see what all the fuss was about.'

'What is the fuss about?'

'I can't quite see, myself. I must be too out of touch. Or too dim. Or both.'

'Well, you know what they say about contemporary English fiction.'

'What do they say?'

'It's no good.'

Flora laughed. 'I believe there's another *they*,' she said, 'who seem to think it's absolutely brilliant.'

'It's as much as their livelihoods are worth to say so,' said Simon.

'Maybe,' said Flora, sadly. 'But they could still be right, couldn't they?'

'No,' said Simon. 'That is, they could be, but they're not. What about that one, what's it about?'

'Adultery,' said Flora.

It was remarkable how, with his head swimming – as if a great red wave had suddenly engulfed it – he was able to converse as if nothing, absolutely nothing, were amiss. Once you've had the education, the words simply speak themselves. 'Adultery, eh?' said Simon, never missing a beat. 'Hasn't that been done before? *The Golden Bowl* comes to mind.'

'As does *A Handful of Dust*.'

'There you are then. That's enough adultery.'

'But as you see, it apparently isn't.'

'Never mind the apparent; I'm concerned solely with the actual.'

Flora put down the book; she did not even keep her

place. She looked at Simon. 'Well, actually,' she said, 'I would have thought that there was everything – or almost everything – still to be said about adultery. The moral landscape has changed radically since Henry James wrote his famous masterpiece. Or Evelyn Waugh his.'

'The change in the moral landscape,' said Simon, 'if I understand correctly the change to which you refer – '

'Well, basically,' said Flora, 'no one, now, actually cares.'

'Not much scope there, then, for a novel,' said Simon. 'Much less a masterpiece.'

'No one, of course, writes masterpieces any more, either,' said Flora. 'Come to that.'

'No, they don't, do they?' said Simon brightly.

'And that's probably a function of the moral landscape too. No one cares.'

'I wonder.'

'Do you?'

'Do you?'

'I don't count,' said Flora. 'My caring is statistically insignificant.' She noted but did not pursue Simon's evasion of her question. Simon could not be expected to care; and she did not want to hear him affirming nevertheless that he did so, even less saying plainly that he did not: for in any case, neither assertion could justly have represented all his true response to such a question. The question itself was too bald, for Simon. He had been right, she saw, to evade it. She was not sure, really, why she had asked it. Of course, he would have cared if he had discovered her, Flora, to be having an adulterous liaison. At the thought of such an eventuality Flora smiled.

'What are you smiling at,' said Simon.

'I was just wondering,' said Flora, 'how any normal person can ever find the time for adultery.'

'Oh,' said Simon. Delirium overtook him, but his tone betrayed no hint of it. 'Needs must, when the devil drives.'

'Ah, the devil,' said Flora. 'I was forgetting the devil.'

'You, of all people,' said Simon.

'Yes,' said Flora. 'Silly, isn't it?'

'No,' said Simon, stricken. 'It does you credit.' Oh God. Oh Flora. Pray for me.

71

'It's been ages, ages.'

'Has it?'

'You know it has.'

'I really wouldn't have thought so.'

'Damn you then.'

'Could you rephrase that?'

He let go of her and walked over to the fireplace. There was an engraved invitation sitting on the mantelpiece; he glanced cursorily at the copperplate. Beside it lay an unfamiliar gold cigarette lighter which he picked up briefly. Cartier. For God's sake. 'Whose vulgar bauble is this?' he said.

'None of your business.'

'Could you rephrase that?'

'What's it to you?'

'I'm a director. Details like that are significant. What sort of person buys a cigarette lighter from Cartier? You do see how preposterous it is, don't you?'

'*Chacun à son goût.*'

'Oh, so it is an *un*, then, is it?'

She sat down. 'I'm autonomous,' she said. 'You're autonomous. You know why you're here. I know why you're here. Let's get on with it, or else – '

He turned away from the fireplace and faced her again. 'Yes,' he said. 'Let's get on with it.'

'This is going wrong, isn't it?' she said, staring at him, baffled.

His heart seemed to contract. 'No,' he said, almost wildly. 'Not a bit of it. Not at all. It was never better. I'm just – I work pretty hard, you know. *Did* you know that?'

'I dare say you do,' she agreed, mildly. 'After all, so do I. Did *you* know *that*?' He looked down at her. You could never quite get used to the idea that women – the women you desired, the women you dreamed of, the women you made love to – actually worked, even worked hard: could actually be compared in this respect to men. Not until you saw them actually working; actually working hard. He looked around the room.

'Yes,' he said. 'I suppose you do, at that.' This lot had to be paid for somehow. She sat back against the sofa cushions, her arms folded, staring up at him, her gaze as candid as a child's. As Solomon's. After a moment he sat down near her. 'I'm sorry,' he said. 'You were quite right. It was none of my business.'

'It belongs to a friend of Albie's,' she said. 'Bloody Albie told him to look me up – he was here for a week on business. He took me to the theatre. Then he came in for a nightcap, and he left that thing behind. It's a fucking nuisance, because I'm going to have to send it after him.'

He was silent, picturing the episode. 'Just stick it in a jiffy bag,' he said. 'It's no big deal.'

'It will be if he doesn't get it,' she said. 'Being as it's so valuable. No, someone will have to go to the Post Office in person and register it. That's the drag of it.'

'I didn't think Americans smoked, these days,' he said.

'No, they don't,' she agreed. 'But you see, he's Venezuelan. Works on Wall Street.'

'What play did you see?' he asked.

'*The Wind in the Willows*,' she replied. It was too delicious. 'He didn't seem to understand it at all. So to speak.' 'Poor Gillian,' he said. She smiled, and shrugged. 'It's all in a day's work.' Oh my darling, my darling. He stood up and, leaning over her, took her hand. 'Come upstairs,' he murmured. She got up and they went upstairs, hand in hand. Nothing was wrong. It was never better. 'What about this cookery, then,' he said afterwards. 'Still at it?'

'I should say so.'

'What if I were to call in on – say – Friday evening? Would you be free?'

She stared up at the ceiling for a moment. 'Friday,' she said. 'No. I'm sorry. Friday's no good.'

'Ah,' he said. 'Right.' Why not? It was none of his business. 'I'm going away for the weekend,' she said.

'That's nice.'

'I hope so.'

He looked at her face, but could read nothing from it. There was no hint of anticipation or of pleasure, of anxiety or of apprehension, or even of boredom. Nothing. 'What about Monday, then,' he said. 'Is that possible?'

She considered the notion for a while. 'It should be,' she said.

He half sat up, leaning on one elbow. 'How soon can you get here,' he said. 'Is six o'clock too early?'

She considered again. This appointment-making, this time-fixing, was not their habitual way. 'I'll try,' she said. 'I can't really promise.'

He lay back again. 'No,' he said. 'Naturally not.'

She turned her head and looked at his profile. 'Why don't you go to the brasserie at six,' she said, 'and I'll meet you there, just as early as I can. It shouldn't be too much later than six.'

'Alright,' he said. 'Yes, okay, I'll do that.'

'Good,' she said. And she turned her head back again, and stared at the ceiling once more, watching the slithering columns of light as the cars passed in the street below.

72

'Was Jesus really real?'

'So they say.'

'They might be lying.'

'That's always possible.'

'What if they *are* lying?'

'He might still be real.'

'How could he be, if they're only lying?'

'You must concentrate. Can you do that?'

'Yes.'

'Alright then. Don't you see that it's possible to say something that's true, even though you yourself don't actually believe that it's true, and are simply lying? For instance, if I say that Thomas is five, when I actually believe he's only four – '

'I'm not! I'm five!'

'Yes, so you are – *we* know that; but if someone who didn't know you were five, and thought you were four, said that you were five, they'd be lying, wouldn't they? From their point of view, that is.'

'Because they were saying something they didn't believe,' said Nell helpfully.

'Exactly,' said Flora. 'But the point here is, that although they were lying, from their point of view, they were still saying something that was true: because Thomas *is* five. Do you see?'

'Why would they think I'm four?' said Thomas.

'Because you're only little,' said Nell.

'I'm not!' said Thomas. 'I'm five!'

'Cripes,' said Flora.

'But what if they're lying,' said Nell, 'and it still isn't true?'

'What isn't true?' said Flora.

'About Jesus,' said Nell,

'Ah,' said Flora. 'Then we have a problem.'

'So what if he isn't real,' Nell persisted. 'What if it's all a real lie?'

'And equally,' said Flora, 'what if he is real, and it's all true?'

'Well, how can you tell,' said Nell, 'whether Jesus is really real, or not, then?'

'You have to see for yourself,' said Flora. 'Each of us has to make up her own mind. Yes, Thomas, or *his*. That, as a matter of fact, is the whole point. One has to decide for oneself, as best one can.'

'What do you think?' said Nell.

'I haven't entirely decided,' said Flora.

'Then why do you go to church?'

'To help me to decide.'

'Do you *have* to decide?' said Nell.

'On the whole,' Flora replied, 'I do believe one does. One way or the other.'

'Why?' said Nell.

'Because,' said Flora, 'there are two possible worlds, the one in which Jesus is real, and the one in which he is not, and it actually does matter which of these two worlds you believe you're living in.'

'Why?' said Nell.

'That is another of those questions you have to think

about for yourself,' said Flora. 'If I gave you my own answer, it would be cheating.'

'When do I have to decide?' said Nell.

'Whenever you can,' said Flora. 'But probably not until you're a fair bit older, actually.'

'That's good,' said Nell. 'Can we go skating after lunch, Mum?'

'We'll see,' said Flora. 'We'll see how your father feels.'

'I'll go and ask him,' said Nell.

'And you can tell him that lunch is almost ready,' said Flora.

But Simon happened to come into the kitchen at this juncture, in quest of the gin. 'Time for a quick pre-prandial?' he asked Flora. Nell put her proposal before him. Of all the appalling ideas: the Queensway ice-rink. But then he remembered that Gillian was away this weekend. The idea was still fairly appalling nevertheless. He bit on the bullet. 'Okay,' he said. 'But no falling over and breaking any bones, okay? I just couldn't stand the hassle.'

Janey came in, and learned what was afoot. 'Can Amaryllis and Katie come too?' she asked.

'Oh, I suppose so,' said Simon with mock weariness. She went away to telephone each of them and returned with the news that Amaryllis, but not Katie, would be of the party; when could she expect to be collected from her home in Holland Park? Simon gave Janey a time and she returned to the telephone. What an absolutely bloody brilliant father I am, thought Simon. And he meant it, every word.

73

'Here I am.'

'At last.'

'I got here as soon as I could.'

'Of course. Do you want anything?'

'I might as well, since I'm here. Just a spritzer, I think.'

'Coming up.' Simon signalled a waiter, and gave the order.

'I see you're on the hard stuff,' said Gillian.

'Simon took another swallow. 'Hard liquor,' he said, 'for a hard man.'

'Golly,' said Gillian. 'You don't say so.'

After they had finished their drinks and left the brasserie, and gone back to the house, and made love, he lay on his back and watched the columns of light sliding across the bedroom ceiling. I will never forget this, he thought. 'Is everything alright?' he asked her.

'Yes, everything's just fine,' she said. And he thought, it's true, isn't it? Everything is just fine. We understand each other. We know what we're doing. It's rare, that is: knowing what one's doing. We've come through, he thought; we've made it. Equilibrium had been achieved. He glanced at the time: if he left now he might just catch Thomas. He stirred.

She came downstairs with him; as he passed the doorway to the sitting room he noticed Rupert's orchid, still blooming. 'Is that thing on steroids?' he said.

She laughed. 'Orchids do furnish a room,' she said. And he suddenly apprehended – or believed he apprehended – how sparse, truly, her life was; how much, how utterly she needed him in it: because who else, truly, cared for her? Who else truly furnished her life? Rupert? Surely not. He was suddenly convinced that he was the only person really in her life, her only chance of an authentic connection.

He put his arms around her. 'Friday?' he said.

'I may be held up,' she said. 'Why don't we meet in the brasserie again – can you do that? Six-thirty-ish?'

'I'll be there,' he said.

74

'Everything okay?'

'Yes, everything's okay. Ish.'

'Perhaps you'd better be precise.'

'Wasn't I?'

'Insufficiently so.'

Flora shrugged. 'What more would you like to know?' she said.

'Well,' said Simon, 'the difference between okay, and okayish, would do to be going on with.'

'I would have thought,' Flora replied, 'that it was fairly obvious that getting home in time to see Thomas is okay, and not doing so is ish: okay?'

'Ish,' said Simon.

Flora stopped stitching and looked up at him. 'Perhaps *you'd* better be precise,' she said.

Simon sighed. 'Oh, God,' he said.

Flora started stitching again. 'Oh God our help in ages past, Our hope for years to come,' she sang; 'Our shelter from the stormy blast, And our eternal home.' She couldn't remember the words of the next verse, so she simply hummed, continuing to stitch the while. Simon stared at her, half irritated and half bemused, and sensing at last his irritation if not his bemusement she let the tune trail away and looked up again. 'By the way,' she said, 'you haven't forgotten about Friday, have you?'

'Friday?'

'Yes, that thing of Lydia's, the private view.'

'The *what*?'

'You know, I told you – the invitation's up there, somewhere. One of her mother's painters is having his first London show. Some gallery in Mayfair – I've forgotten which; it's up there anyway. You said we might go along – surely you remember?'

'You don't want to go to a thing like that!'

'But I *do*. It would be fun.'

'Honestly, Flora, what on earth's got into you? A lot of lousy modern paintings, unspeakable people and undrinkable Chablis – you've got to be kidding.' Flora said nothing, her face averted over her work. 'Aren't you?' said Simon.

'No,' she said. 'I thought it might be fun. It would be a change. We never go anywhere like that.'

'Too right we don't. It's not even as if we like modern paintings.'

'It's not just the paintings,' said Flora. 'And anyway, Lydia could use a bit of moral support. After all, she's more or less obliged to be there, but she won't know anyone, except this painter chap, whom she's only just met, if that much.'

Simon sighed. 'Bloody Lydia,' he said, but without force. Flora gave him a look but said nothing. 'Well look,' he went on, 'why don't you go along without me, then?'

'Oh!' cried Flora, 'but that wouldn't be nearly the same.'

Simon sighed again. 'I'm sorry, sweetheart,' he said; as if he meant it. And he all but did. 'I really can't manage it – not Friday. Not as it looks from here. What time's the off? Six to eight sort of thing, eh? It's impossible. You go along without me.'

'I'll see,' said Flora in a small voice. 'I'll see if Louisa's going, or Claire.'

'There you are,' said Simon. 'One of them's bound to be, if not both. You girls get stuck in there. You'll enjoy it much more without me.'

'I won't,' said Flora.

75

Simon was sitting with his back to the door when Lydia, with half an hour to kill in between visiting her Bayswater photographer and going on to the private view, came into the brasserie.

And Lydia, having taken so long earlier in the afternoon to dress for the occasion, apprehensive about it in any case, sitting down in the nearest available place – at a table near the door – wasn't tempted, alone and self-conscious as she felt, to look around her, and might not have recognised Simon's rear view if she had, but ordered a filter coffee (she didn't want to mix her drinks) and lit a cigarette, and then stared out of the window at the passing crowd. This is the place I saw Simon and that blonde woman coming into that night, she thought.

And this was the moment, precisely, when she saw the woman herself entering the brasserie once again. For as Lydia herself had often quite carelessly observed (never quite believing it, in all its depth and import) London is a karmic sort of place. She watched, frozen, as the woman crossed the room; she saw, horrified, that the man who rose to greet her was Simon.

Her heart was still thumping as she sat in the taxi which was taking her to the private view; she still all but trembled with the shock. Their heads together, their hands clasped – there could be no doubt now that they were lovers: she, Lydia, had witnessed this thing.

There had been the woman's apparent awareness of her furtive glances – which had consequently ceased; and at last there had been the worst thing of all, when, as she was leaving – casting one last almost involuntary glance in their direction – she had caught, very briefly, Simon's eye in the mirror opposite which he was sitting.

She had looked away instantly, pretending utter obliviousness – acting the complete and disinterested stranger – and, having paid her bill, had sailed out of the brasserie, her back as straight as a rod, her head held high, sublimely, apparently, unaware; but trembling with shock, and even fright, her heart thumping, her mind in a daze. God, oh God, she was saying to herself; oh, God. She was still saying this, dazedly looking through the window, as her taxi bore her down Park Lane, the Friday night traffic loud and frantic all around her, the park a lake of black silence in the distance beyond.

76

'And who, *exactly*, is Lydia Faraday?'

Simon was still quite pale with dismay. To have been seen – bad; but to have seen himself being seen – vile. An eventuality so dreadful that its import must be denied.

'She's no one, absolutely no one.'

'Come now.'

'No, truly. She's just a person Flora – just someone Flora knew at Cambridge. She's no one.'

'All the same.'

He took her hand again. 'All the same, nothing. I mean, she won't say anything, or – anything.'

'Are you quite sure about that?'

The thing was, Gillian seemed quite calm now. She leaned back and lit a cigarette; she was looking at him quite coolly; he could even have said that she did not entirely (or at all) believe him; that she was interrogating him. 'Of course I am,' he said impatiently. 'I tell you, she's no one. In any case, what did she see? Nothing.'

'She saw us.'

'What of it?'

'Don't you wonder what we looked like to her, sitting here?'

Simon was silent. His head was still swimming; he couldn't think straight.

'I'm afraid,' said Gillian, very slowly, 'that we've had it, my dear.'

It was too dreadful to be credible. 'Don't be absurd,' said Simon.

'You really don't quite understand, do you?'

'Understand *what?*'

'What this really *means*. To have been seen, like this.'

'As I keep saying, she saw nothing. I'll fix her. Of course it's an awful drag, but I'll fix her.'

'You mean you'll tell her some plausible story.'

'Nothing to it.'

'You really *don't* see, do you?'

'See *what?*'

'That having to tell *some plausible story* is as bad as bad can get. You know, never apologise, never explain – once you start doing either, it's all up. I'm sorry. But it really is.'

And now at last he saw, hidden behind her apparent calm, beyond her relentless questions, the shock from which she too was suffering. He was appalled. 'Let's for God's sake get out of here,' he muttered; and they went back to her house, both silent and terrified of the pass they had reached. Here it finally is, Simon thought, as they walked down the early-evening lamplit street: here is the abyss. 'Cold tonight, isn't it?' he said pointlessly. Inside the house they clung to each other and made love passionately, but it was no good; it really was no good; they both knew this, but it had become unthinkable that either should say so. 'Don't worry,' said Simon. 'I'll fix old Lydia.'

'Yes,' Gillian said wearily. 'No.'

77

Dazed, trembling, still – here now she was. Quickly, out on the pavement – pay the cabbie – go inside: never mind anything – grab a drink. Not the inferior Chablis foreseen by Simon, but a reliable South Australian Riesling. Well, naturally.

Here were all the usual liggers, all merrily talking their heads off, God bless them. She heard her mother's voice in her ear, six years old, felt the maternal hand on her back: 'You're *on*, darling'; she felt the heat of the sudden bright lights after the nervous darkness of the wings. She was on, another bit-player, with all the self-consciousness of a star. She drank another mouthful of wine. The shock was subsiding and a light-headed febrility was beginning to take its place.

If only she hadn't caught Simon's eye – if only that. But if only she hadn't, she wouldn't, as she now did, *know*. And what she *knew* was too dreadful to contain. Here she was, nonetheless, containing it – so she supposed. Simon's guilty glance: Simon's found-out glance. Oh, Simon. Not simply wicked (if you wanted to be old-fashioned) but careless. Another mouthful, before she did her stuff here, and – oh, God. There was Flora.

'Flora!'

'We were afraid you weren't coming!'

'And Janey too! How nice.'

'Simon couldn't come, so I thought – '

'Yes, *what* a good idea. Have you looked at the paintings yet? What do you think, Janey? Are they any good?'

'You can't see them properly, there are too many people in the way.'

'How true. Oh, there's Claire. See over there, talking to Will Feather.'

'Yes, we know – she ditched us for Mr Feather.'

'Well, Claire has her row to hoe. That reminds me, I should hoe my own, I must pay my respects to the artist. I wonder which he is.' Lydia looked around at all the English faces; it was hopeless.

'I think that's him over there,' said Janey. Lydia looked: Janey was probably right.

'Excuse me a moment,' she said. It was indeed he: as she came closer she heard the quacking of antipodean vowels. She waited for a break and introduced herself. 'How nice to meet you at last,' she said. She was two glasses of wine down; was she overdoing it? 'Gidday,' said the antipodean amiably, 'likewise.' 'Well – ' said Lydia, 'they've certainly got a crowd in tonight. Everyone's here.'

'Yeah, it's beaut!'

'I'm afraid I haven't had a chance yet to see the paintings properly – so many people in the way.'

'No worries; they'll be up for two more weeks.'

'Yes, I must come back during the day.'

'You do that.'

'Yes. Anyway, I do hope you're enjoying London – but then I dare say you've been here before.'

'Oh yeah, I have; it's bonzer.'

'Oh good.'

'Yeah, I've been havin' a beaut time.'

'Oh, beaut. Oh, sorry – I mean – '

'No worries!'

'Oh good. Anyway – where are you staying exactly?'

'Oh, I've got a loan of a triffic flat in Notting Hill.'

'Oh yes, Notting Hill.'

'Yeah that's right – beaut place.'

'So you know lots of people here, do you?'

'Oh, well, I know a few. I've met some more here. They're bonzer people.'

'Oh, are they?'

'Yeah, right; triffic!'

'Well, some friends of mine are here tonight who'd love to meet you – Claire Maclise, just over there – you see – '

'Oh yeah, I've met her already; she's beaut.'

'Yes, I'm sure she'd adore to know you'd said that, I must tell her – '

'You beauty.'

'And then there's darling Flora, just over there, Flora Beaufort – see, with the *jeune fille en fleur*, well, almost – '

'Oh yeah I noticed her. Bonzer, isn't she?'

'Yes, she is; as a matter of fact she's rather clever, too, you know; she's at St Paul's.'

'Oh yeah? That's triffic.'

'Yes, it is actually. Anyway, come and meet her, and Flora too.'

'Righty-oh; that'll be beaut!'

78

'Where were you?'

'Honestly, Simon. At that private view, remember?'

'For God's sake.'

'Did you pay the baby-sitter?'

'Yes of course I did.'

'Good. Well, let's have some stew. Could you light the gas under it Janey? Not too high. You haven't eaten yet have you Simon?'

'No, I was waiting for you.'

'How sweet.'

'Well, did you enjoy yourselves?'

'Yes, it was *beaut*.'

Flora and Janey both started to laugh. Simon looked from one to the other. They tried to explain the joke but he didn't seem to appreciate it. 'Honestly,' said Flora, 'he was just so funny. It was ages before we cottoned on that he was putting it all on. Well, quite a lot. Playing the Australian card. Really funny. What a shame you couldn't come. It really was bonzer.' Flora put the casserole of stew on the table, and they sat down to eat. 'He thinks Janey's beaut, too,' she went on. 'He said, that's a real beaut little girl you've got there, Flora.'

'How much did you have to drink?' said Simon.

'Oh, listen to you,' said Flora. Knives were turning constantly in Simon's stomach. He did not see how life was to be endured. He suddenly realised that he was going to go and see Lydia: he was going to fix Lydia, somehow. He must go and see her first thing tomorrow. It was the only landing he could make, as he fell, farther and farther, into the nightmare. The knives turned more slowly, then were still. Oh, but the agony. 'Lydia was looking nice, didn't you think, Janey?'

'She looked okay,' said Janey. 'Not real beaut, but okay.'

'She looked *beaut*,' said Flora firmly, and they laughed again. Simon could have shouted at them; he ate some more stew. 'She was wearing a rather beaut hat,' said Flora. 'She got it in the Harrods sale. It's French.'

'Jolly good,' said Simon. 'Beaut.'

'No, but you know,' said Flora, 'talking of hat faces, I know she isn't beautiful, but she has got a hat face, Lydia has. She can wear a hat.'

'Good-oh,' said Simon.

'Anyway, it was all a lot of fun,' said Flora. 'You should have come.'

'Yes,' said Simon. 'It serves me right.'

'There you go,' said Flora.

'Yes,' said Simon. 'I do that.' And he found that the knives had started, slowly at first, and then with increasing speed, to turn again in his stomach. The pain was just unspeakable.

Flora stretched. 'Let's watch a funny film,' she said. 'I feel like laughing.' And she smiled happily at Simon, who, while he could have wept, smiled, nay grinned, heroically back.

'Yes,' he said. 'Why not?'

79

'I suppose you know why I've come here.'

'Yes; I should think I probably do.' Lydia stood quite still, her arms folded, and looked at Simon's drawn face, and waited. Simon shrugged slightly, and looked down at the floor. He was helpless. What, now, to say? What, in God's name, to say?

'This room looks different from the last time I was here.' Didn't it, though. And yet, there was something – one thing – that was jarringly familiar: why?

The walls were all painted a sort of greyish-lilac, with cream woodwork, and the floor was covered with some sort of seagrass matting. Cream calico curtains, hanging to the floor; a deck-chair with a white canvas seat; a glass coffee table – its legs seemed to be made of glass, too: they must be perspex. A sort of luxurious austerity, summed up exactly by the long leather and chrome sofa. Simon felt almost faint: the world had turned suddenly backwards on its axis. 'New sofa, isn't it?' he said. A sort of terror had seized him.

Lydia looked over at the sofa and smiled faintly. 'Oh yes, that,' she said. 'Handsome, isn't it? Got it in an auction sale. There were actually two, but I thought one ought to be enough.'

'Absolutely.'

Of all uncanny connections. It was intolerable. His head was swimming. Lydia made a gesture. 'Well, do sit down,' she said. 'It's entirely functional.' Simon, very slowly, sat. If he were to lift the cushions, he thought, he would be quite sure to find at least one of Solomon's hairs. Lydia took pity at last. 'Coffee?' she said; she went into the kitchen and switched on the kettle.

When the coffee was served she sat down on the deck-chair and lit a cigarette. 'Well,' she said.

Simon had not rehearsed what he should say. The only way, last night, all night, this morning, to still those turning knives had been to assure himself that he really could fix Lydia. That he – they – could in some way return to the *status quo ante*. What, after all, had she seen?

'Odd that you should have run into us last night, at that place.'

'Not really. I'm quite often in the neighbourhood.'

'I didn't know that.'

'I suppose if you had, I mightn't have run into you.'

'Possibly not.'

'One can't be too careful.'

He said nothing.

'As it is . . .'

'You probably want an explanation.'

'I'm not entirely sure that I do. Everything seems fairly clear, doesn't it?'

'Everything?'

'Well, there you were, with another woman, with whom you are evidently on terms of some intimacy – '

'You're quite sure about that, are you?'

'More or less.'

'It wouldn't do to be too hasty.'

'No, that's what I told myself, too, at one stage. At first, of course, I was entirely sure.' She wouldn't bother, she thought, to tell him about her earlier sighting. 'But after the shock – as it were – wore off, and after I'd been back in the world – so to speak – for a few hours, I began to wonder. As one does. I did see that there might be an alternative reading.'

'Or even several such.'

'One is enough.'

'True. There we are then. I wouldn't like to think you'd gone off with the wrong impression.'

'Then you'd better make quite sure I've got the right one.'

'You imply that I actually owe it to you.'

'You implied as much yourself by coming here.'

There was a silence; Simon drank some coffee. Lydia looked at her watch. 'I haven't very much more time,' she murmured. 'I've got to meet this painter chap at the Tate. He wants to show me the Wattses.'

'The Wattses,' Simon repeated stupidly.

'Yes, you know. *Hope*, and so on. He says Watts is the coming man.'

'He's dead.'

'Still coming though. Vastly underrated, this chap says. Very important painter. Coming like no one's business.'

'I'll drop you off.'

'Ah. Should I accept?'

'Think about it,' said Simon drily. 'In the meantime – '

'You still have a problem.'

'Have I?'

'Inasmuch as I may still be labouring under a misconception.'

'No,' said Simon. 'I'm quite happy, as long as you see that you may be. As long as we're clear that nothing, after all, is clear.'

'Is that really good enough?'

'Isn't it?'

'And even if it were, I'm not quite sure, after all, that it really is so.'

'Ah.'

'Because, you see,' and Lydia's voice became quite gentle, 'if it weren't quite clear — clear enough, that is — then you wouldn't, after all, have come here.'

'Would I not?'

'No, I'm afraid you really would not. Only a guilty conscience would have brought you here.'

'Not simple anxiety?'

'No. There wouldn't even have been any anxiety, you see. Not you.'

Simon considered these statements. 'You're probably right,' he said. 'So . . .' Lydia went on, 'the fact is — sorry to be so crude, but needs must — you have apparently been having a liaison with this woman, and you've been found out; and now you want to know what I'm going to do.'

'I hadn't really thought you'd do anything, actually.'

'I wouldn't tell Flora?'

'No, you wouldn't do that.'

'I'd keep your secret, then.'

'When you put it like that — '

'That is what it amounts to.'

'Alright. I suppose it does.'

'That I, Lydia, should keep your secret — '

'Yes, it is rather much. I do see that.'

'It's a little too much. I won't undertake to keep it altogether, however. Only to keep it from Flora.'

Simon was silent, speechless, for now, at the sight of all these appalling implications. 'There is of course something you'll have to do in return,' said Lydia. 'Or rather, in fact, for its own sake.'

'What's that?' It could only get worse, couldn't it?

'Stop seeing her.'

'I can't do that.'

'Don't be pathetic.'

'I can't.'

'Don't be stupid. You can, and you will. Pretend this is wartime, and one of you has been killed. Do whatever you have to. Seriously. You have no choice. Whatever it was, it's finished. Do you understand? I'm willing to keep your secret of past folly, but not of a present and continuing folly. To say no worse. It's out of the question – I'm sure you see that.'

Simon was silent. He saw.

Lydia sat up straight. 'I'm glad that's sorted out,' she said. 'Oh, just one thing – who is she?'

Simon, shattered, ruined, in shreds, looked pitifully down at his hands. 'Her name is Gillian Selkirk,' he said. 'She's an accountant, she works in the City. I met her during the summer, when Flora and the kids were in France.' He was watching his past unwinding like a film before him, a drowning man: Camden Town; David and Sarah; Gillian Selkirk; the mansion flat; Solomon; everything.

'Well,' said Lydia, almost harshly, 'chalk it up to experience, Simon. You were careless. Or perhaps foolhardy is the better word. Whatever. Look, I must get ready now and be off.'

Simon looked up, his eyes dull. 'Shall I give you a lift, then?' he said. 'It's only fair, when I've kept you.'

'No,' said Lydia. 'It's alright. I'll just make it if I get going now.'

'Yes,' said Simon, 'right, okay.' He got up. She went to the door with him. Here she inexplicably touched his arm, and he as inexplicably turned to her and put a hand on her shoulder. She looked dispassionately at his drawn face.

'Take care, Simon,' she said. 'You utter creep.'

'You take care too,' he said. 'You – Lydia.' Then he was gone. Lydia sighed, and began to get ready. What to wear? Ah yes. Men, she thought; men are just *pathetic*. But – well. There we are.

80

'I had lunch with Lydia today.'

'Good show.'

'I say, Robert?'

'Louisa?'

'I suppose you've never come across an accountant named Gillian Selkirk, have you?'

'Shouldn't say I have. Accountants are not really my sort of thing.'

'Well, no, but I just thought, the City – '

'Big place. Many mansions.'

'She's a blonde.'

'I believe they quite often are.'

'She's the woman Simon Beaufort has been having an affair with.'

'The naughty little thing. Shall I report her to the Institute of Chartered Accountants? Anonymously, of course.'

'Robert, do be serious.'

'Is that really necessary?'

'Think of Flora.'

'That's another matter altogether. I was thinking – as I supposed you intended I should – of the accountant Selkirk. Does Flora actually know?'

'Good God no. And she never must. I'm relying on your discretion absolutely. Obviously.'

'Absolutely. Obviously.'

'I think Simon is an utter creep.'

'We-e-ell – *utter* is a bit strong, perhaps.'

'Lydia told him so, too.'

'Now where exactly does Lydia come into all this?'

'Don't you remember? She saw them, that time I told you about. And it turns out you were right, after all, because on Friday night she saw them again, and all is now revealed.' And Louisa brought Robert up to date, with a rational account of the events of Friday evening and Saturday morning. 'So there it is,' she said. 'Ghastly, isn't it?'

Robert considered. 'Well, ghastlyish,' he said. 'Still, as long as it's all over.'

'Well, we have only Simon's word for that.'

'Have to trust the chap.'

'No earthly reason why we should.'

'Nevertheless.'

'Hmmm.'

'*Flora*,' Robert said.

'Yes, Flora,' said Louisa. 'Of all people.'

'What she doesn't know can't hurt her.'

'You know perfectly well that it can.'

'I was really just trying it out to see how it sounded.'

'And it sounds like rubbish. Everything is changed now, forever.'

'Everything changes, all the time: forever. All the time. No matter what.'

'I suppose so.'

'Believe me.'

'Alright.'

'The wind bloweth where it listeth.'

'Whoo-oo-oo,' said Louisa. 'Whoo-oo, whoo-oo.'

Robert smiled at her. He had worked conscientiously for all the other glittering prizes he had won, but Louisa had come like a falling star into his hand unbidden, unforeseen; he would never quite believe his luck. '*Whoo-oo!*' he replied. 'Look, it's nearly half-past: shall we watch *Newsnight?*'

81

'What is it – oh – tea – I say – ' Simon sat up, still half asleep:
oh, those knives. The grey day. 'Thank you,' he said.

Flora put the tea beside him. 'I thought I'd better wake
you,' she said. 'It's past ten o'clock; you mightn't have been
able to sleep tonight.'

'Aren't you going to church?'

'No, not today.' She sat down on the low chair by the
window. She looked at him. 'I don't have to go every single
Sunday,' she said. 'I mean, one wouldn't want to overdo it.'

'God forbid.'

'Are you feeling quite alright, Simon?'

'Yes, I'm fine; never better.'

He had gone to see Gillian straight away – that is, after a
long time of sitting by the canal, on a bench on the towpath,
watching the water rippling in the biting winter breeze. He
hadn't telephoned first. There she'd been, in an apron,
cooking. Pleased and happy. He'd soon put a stop to that.
She had sat down at the kitchen table, leaning her arms on
it. 'It's alright,' she had said. 'Truly. It's alright. Something
like this was bound to happen, it always is. Nothing's ever
any good; not really. Not forever. No, don't worry about
me: I'm fine. Please don't worry. Look, I must get on.
Rupert and I are giving a dinner party – see – he's going to
do the steak *au poivre*, and I'm doing the *gratin dauphinois*:
and I'm making this pudding as a surprise. He doesn't know

about that, he thinks we're just having biscuits and cheese afterwards. See?' There was an illustration in the *Larousse gastronomique* open on the table. 'And I must get on now,' she said. 'Or it won't be a surprise.' And he saw everything that was wrong, and had always been, with them – with her, with him, with it – from the start. But he wouldn't not have had it for the world, because he truly, so far as he could understand the phenomenon, loved her. And now this suffering: and hers. Oh God: hers, too.

Not that he didn't love Flora. Not that he loved Flora, now or at any time, any the less.

'You look so whacked. Poor darling – I'm afraid you've been overdoing it.'

'Do you think so?'

'You're always like this at this stage of a production.'

'Am I?'

'Always.'

'What a drag for you.'

'I don't mind for myself. Look, I was thinking we might have an early lunch, and then go to the Tate.'

'What a bizarre idea.'

'Yes, it's not bad, is it? But I think Janey's got something else on with the eternal Amaryllis, so it's just Thomas and Nell. Do you want to come along?'

'I dunno.'

'No, do. It will refresh your spirit.'

'Oh, will it?'

'We're going to look at the Wattses.'

'The Wattses.'

'*Hope*, etcetera. He's the coming man.'

The world spinning backwards again.

'He's dead.'

'Yes, but he's coming nonetheless. That's what Brian says. You know, that painter.'

'These Australians who come here and tell us what's what.'

Flora laughed. 'Actually he did say that an Englishman had got there first; there's a book just coming out.'

'So if we bash round there this afternoon we'll get ahead of the crowd, eh?'

'Yes, that's right. Do come.'

'I'll see.'

Where else should one, could one, go, on this afternoon – Patagonia? So he went with Flora and Thomas and Nell to the Tate Gallery: they dropped Janey off in Holland Park on the way.

Hope was high up on the wall: 'I can't see,' Thomas complained. Simon lifted him up and the child stared at the painting for a minute. 'I don't like her,' he said. 'Put me down.' Simon and Flora, continuing both to contemplate the painting – Nell meanwhile giving every appearance of so doing – each wondered, separately, fleetingly, whether in fact it were something any child should ever see.

'Hmmm,' said Simon at last. 'Yes.'

Flora turned her head towards him. She had been holding Thomas's hand all the while. 'Shall we go and look at something else?' she said.

'Alright,' Simon agreed.

'We'll see if we can find something Thomas will like.'

'And something for me, too,' said Nell in a voice which had only the faintest note of melancholy.

'Of course, darling,' said Flora. 'I'll bet there's something in this very room that you'll like. Walk around it and see, while I wait here for you.'

She sat down and watched Nell's progress until the child

suddenly returned, looking pleased. 'I've found something I like,' she announced. Flora and Thomas went with her to see, and then they walked slowly about finding a picture for Thomas; but Simon continued, after all, now sitting where Flora had, to stare up at Watts's enigmatic work: staring, but no longer truly seeing – or seeing, perhaps, more truly than the naked eye can do: wondering, almost overwhelmed as he was by the consciousness of his devastation, how, and what, to think of himself, now.

Much later, when the children were all in bed, Flora picked up the postcards they had bought before leaving the gallery and looked through them, smiling at Nell's choices, laughing at Thomas's. She came at last to *Hope*, and gazed at the picture again for a time. 'Awfully strange, isn't it?' she murmured.

'Everything is strange, really.'

'Everything is real, strangely.'

Simon laughed, briefly, mirthlessly. 'Yes,' he said. 'It's a wonder how we can actually go on.'

'Well, we simply must, that's all. That, really, or strangely, is *how*. You see – after all, it's all so transitory.'

'Yes,' said Simon; 'but – '

'Yes,' said Flora. 'But.'

And there really seemed no need, at least for the time being, to say another word.